ISBN 978-1-54398-152-0

AF207922

Forbidden Honey Dew Chronicles

Book 2:

Balor's Reign

& The Dungeons of Britnoitula

© 2019 Glade Arthur Swope

fmi: www.GladeSwope.com

This is a work of entertainment fiction. Any similarities to actual persons, places, or events are coincidental.

Prelude:

Meanwhile,

two years later,

in the realm of Malkuth,

also known as

reality,

at least

as most people know it...

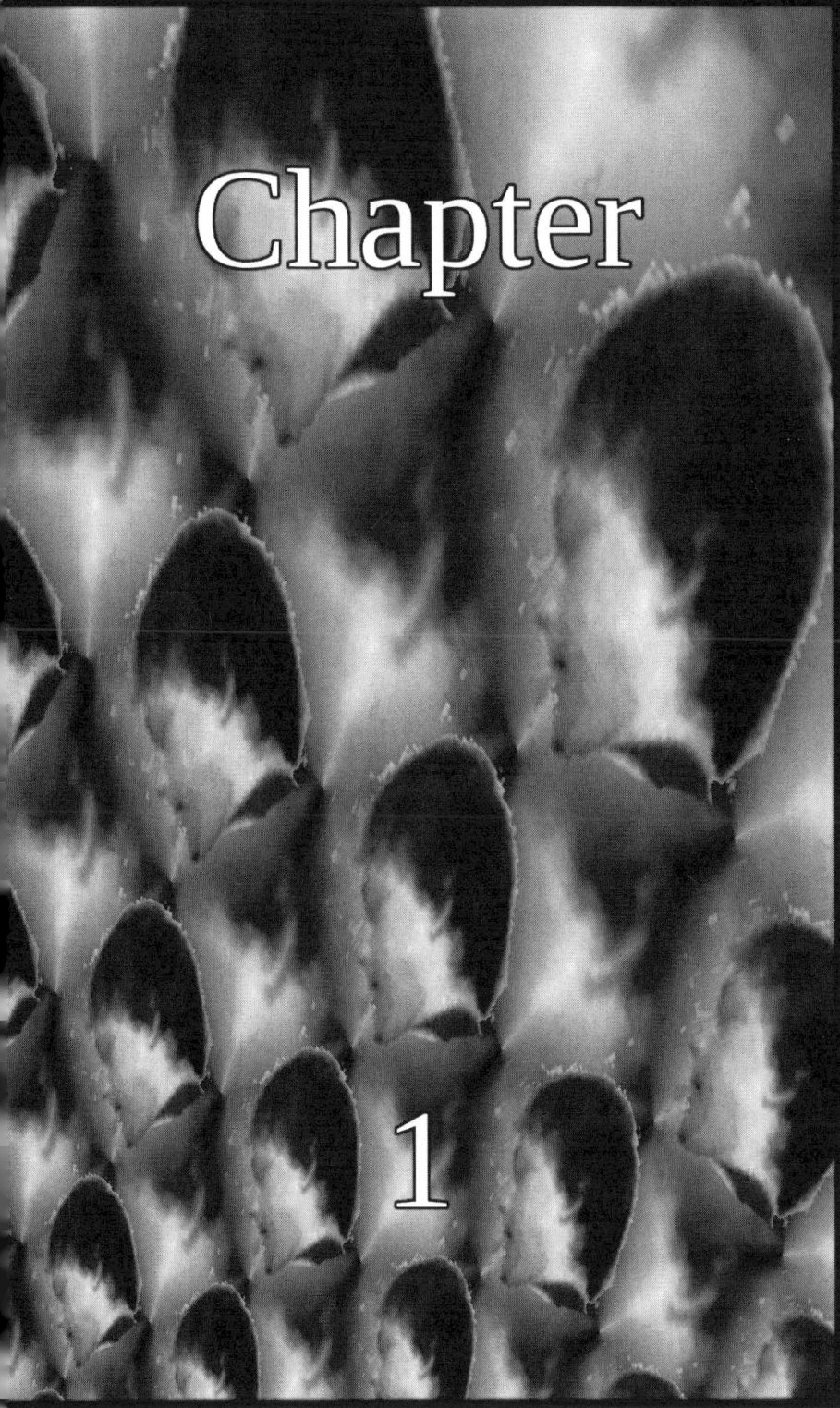

Chapter

1

It is Friday. In a classroom of a public high school, a 17 year old guy studies a book on his desk intently. He looks a bit old for a 17-year-old, his hair gray, and his skin ragged. Parts of his skin are badly burned from tattoo removal surgery. On his backpack, is embroidered his name, "Bill." Everyone is dressed in semi-formal attire, well-pressed. Nobody wears sneakers, as if they lived in the time when you had to sneak around to wear them. It is 8 AM. The bell rings. The class are waiting patiently for the teacher to arrive.

The Ten Commandments are posted on the wall. Next to them is a plaque of three transparent crosses. There is a Norman Rockwell poster relating to a war bond campaign from World War Two on the other side of the room, from the *Four Freedoms* series, *Freedom of Worship*; or, as Bill and his friends would often joke when the teacher isn't watching, "Save Freedom of War Ship; Buy War Bombs." It depicts people praying in a crowd. Being quite sensitive and intelligent, Bill can tell that two lines of text have been removed near the top of the artwork. He can't read it, but knows that there is something very important to the poster's message in the removed text. For Bill was the kind of boy who lacked the ability to ignore his intuition, and it often got the best of him. His mom often said that he had too much attention to detail for his own good. On closer inspection, and deep meditation, for the first time today, Bill can make out one word at the end of the second rubbed out line, "conscience." The lady in the upper right corner of the painting almost seems to be staring at that word. Bill knows that there is more written there. He has been trying to read this extremely faint line of text for years.

A door opens at the back of the room. Almost flinching at the sound of the door opening, Bill hides his book in his backpack and zips it up quickly. The teacher just walked in.

The teacher approaches his desk. He is dressed in thick black pants, white shirt and tie, with an image of three crosses embroidered into the shirt pocket. His forehead is covered by the bangs of his dark black hair, yet the back side of it is at collar, somewhat like a reverse-mullet. He says, "Godly morning and praise the Lord for this day that He has made." He motions his hand to a flag by the desk. It looks like the American flag as of the twentieth century, except that the stars are replaced with crucifixes, and the stripes are detailed as the images of benches. "Now, all will please rise, with all your heart, soul, mind and strength, for the Lord's Prayer, the Pledge of Allegiance, and the Affirmation of The Faith."

Each and everyone stands up, puts one hand on their chest, the other raised. They recite in unison, "Our Father, who art in Heaven, hallowed be Thy name. Thy Kingdom come, Thy will be done, on Earth as it is in Heaven. Give us this day our daily bread. Forgive us our trespasses, as we forgive those who trespass against us. And lead us not into temptation, but deliver us from evil. For thine is the kingdom and the power and the glory forever. Amen. I pledge allegiance to the flag of the *Kingdom of God* of America; And to the Dominion for which it stands, one world nation, under God, with leniency to those that believe and obey to the uttermost, and eternal punishment for all others. There is no God but God, and as proven by fire come down from Heaven, John Adramalech Balor is His prophet. Whosoever does not believe and obey the prophet John Adramalech Balor disobeys God, and shall perish, both of body and of spirit, forever and ever and ever, yea and amen."

Bill silently reflects to himself, "We are often reminded, in this very same class, to say, and write, 'Yes' instead of 'Yea' which is considered slang. It used to be the other way around. After all, if it's good enough for the Bible, ... ?"

The English grammar class sits down and continues uneventfully. Bill gets his assignment done quickly, then he can't stop staring at the rubbed out message at the top of the *Freedom of Worship* painting. Having that one word made out so fresh in his mind, he figures that this is the best time ever to try. For years had Bill pondered what this message, which the powers that be, obviously don't want people to see, is all about.

When the bell rings, everyone gets up quietly. They slowly march out into the hall. They are careful not to speak to each other until they know that there are no staff around.

A boy with yellow hair and brown eyes says, "Hey, Billy, you seemed to be really interested in that book. You were in a hurry to put it away. Did you not want the teacher to see it?"

"Shh. Can't talk about it here, Jay. I'll tell you at

the information rave tonight. I want to come."

"Sure thing."

Billy and Jay split up, headed for different class rooms. Billy quickly uses the bathroom, and on his way out a man approaches and says, "Random search time, William MacDonald Charles."

Shuddering in fear, Billy puts down his backpack.

The man says, "Open it."

Bill hesitates.

The man growls, "Ahem, hiding something?"

The bell rings.

The man says, "Tardy, tar, tar, no tardy-pass for you if I have to open it. You had best save me the trouble, and yours."

Bill opens the backpack, "Nothing here but my books, and my boots. Honest."

The man picks a book out of the backpack. It's Mark Twain's *Adventures of Huckleberry Finn*. "Can't seem to find any boots, but look what we have here! It looks like you've got your hands on some juicy *Class C Subversive Literature*. Hmm..." The man pushes some buttons on his phone, points at Bill with a glare, and shouts, "Don't move a muscle. On your knees."

Bill kneels, "Ut-oh."

The principal storms in, and Bill is escorted to the office. The principal places Bill's copy of *Adventures of Huckleberry Finn* on a cast iron plate mounted on the side of his desk. He lights a match, and drops it on the book. The smoke detector, which is a server model with a built-in console, rings as the book burns. Alarms sound all over the campus. The principal grabs bill by the neck, and holds his left ear up to the smoke detector. He says, "The rest of the school will be having an unexpected fire-" He pulls a cordless drill out of his desk, holds it up to Bill's right ear, pulls the trigger, and it's quite loud. "-drill, but you're still mine for now."

Bill's ears are in serious pain, and he screams, "Enough already!" He grabs the drill and throws it on the floor. He rips the fire alarm server off the wall and throws it on top of the book, putting out the fire.

The principal grabs the partially burned book, and throws it in the trash with angry force. He says, "You know we go to great lengths to prevent people from being deceived, from being led astray from the only true way to redemption. There are many forms of subversive entertainment, many which were considered very respectable and wholesome in the past, back when we were a pluralistic and secular nation, anything goes and all that. Now we are a holy Christian society that has recognized their danger. How did you come about this illegal and dangerous book?"

Bill hesitates before responding. He bought this book at a wild party, but knows not to tell. He says, "I don't remember. It was a long time ago. I was probably sto-, uh, I mean, very tired at the time."

"How much of it have you read?"

Bill had read about half of it, and just got past the part where Huckleberry is threatened that he would not make it to Heaven if he helped the slave escape. Tactfully, careful not to wink an eye, Bill answers, "Only the first fifteen pages."

"Consider yourself fortunate that we caught you when we did. If you had read the story's subversive portion, we would have to hold you for intense orthodox reeducation, lest ye be deceived."

The principal puts the fire alarm console back on the wall, resets it, and speaks into the PA microphone, "All right class, this was only a drill. Please return to your regularly scheduled classes at once. The tardy bell will ring in two minutes."

The bathroom is next to the office, and Bill can hear frantic footsteps, since those who needed to use the bathroom had to run. Anyway, Bill feels like he needs to go to the bathroom again, but is afraid to talk about it.

Bill asks, "How can knowing what's in a classic book be considered being deceived? How am I less deceived by not knowing what happens in a work of fiction?"

"Yes, it was once called classic, but that's just the taste of people of the world. The wisdom of unbelievers must be disregarded, lest we be unequally yoked, and thereby deceived. And, by the way, Mark Twain is, and forever will be, paying for his damnable literary mischief in flames. It's not a matter of knowing enough, but of believing the prophets that God has sent, and obeying their exhortations. When we speak of being deceived, it does not matter how good, bad, or true the information may in fact be. When we speak of being deceived, we speak of anything that tendeth to leadeth our lambs away. Even many portions of our

American history that were once a standard of public education must be forgotten, to restore us to the one true faith."

Bill is immediately reminded of the missing words on the painting. The bell rings.

The principal continues, "Those whom we as a nation once called Founding Fathers, were heretics just as Mark Twain was. Their greatest heresy was known as the separation of Church and St- oh... no... I shouldn't've said that. I... should... not... have... said that." He covers his mouth, nervous for a moment, then continues, "Although some of the knowledge and entertainment works of the world are better than others, and can even be useful to learn virtues from time to time, unless you are extremely careful, it all leads to the same place, the highway to you-know-where. Remember, from the very beginning, it was a tree of knowledge. Not some gross wrongdoing, just knowledge, that led to original sin, and made all to be born damned to eternal life in fire and brimstone unless they find salvation."

"In that case, this is the key question: What do you mean by 'true'?"

The principal pulls a *King James Bible* out of a file cabinet, places it on the desk, and says, "The one standard, at the root of all standards, for truth."

"It all comes down to because we say so?"

"No, it's God saying because He says so through us, and that's that." He hands Bill a red pen, and a sheet of ruled writing paper. He opens the *Bible* and begins to read, "*Matthew* Chapter 15, verses 21 to 28. As a test to your faith, I want to see you write these verses out by hand as I read aloud." He slows his speech to about twenty words per minute, and recites with the *Bible* open in Bill's face, "Then Jesus went thence, and departed into the coasts of Tyre and Sidon. And, behold, a woman of Canaan came out of the same coasts, and cried unto him, saying, Have mercy on me, O Lord, thou son of David; my daughter is grievously vexed with a devil. But he answered her not a word. And his disciples came and besought him, saying, Send her away; for she crieth after us. But he answered and said, I am not sent but unto the lost sheep of the house of Israel. Then came she and worshipped him, saying, Lord, help me. But he answered and said, It is not meet to take the children's bread, and to cast it to dogs. And she said, Truth, Lord: yet the dogs eat of the crumbs which fall from their masters' table. Then Jesus answered and said unto her, 'No one talketh back at the Lord God and live. Thy daughter be vexed with a devil indeed, for she belongs to him. She will surely be cast into Hell forever, along with you likewise unless ye repent of your rebellion.'"

As Bill starts to pen out the last verses, he feels an intense unease. He knows that something is very, very wrong here, but he does not know what it is. When he gets half-way through writing the word "talketh", his wrist shakes. His eyes flinch at the sight of the words in the book. He can't bring himself to continue writing it.

The principal barks, "It's the Word of God whether you like it or not. His thoughts are higher than our thoughts. We must accept all of His judgments, even the ones that feel wrong to you. When you think it's wrong, you're just seeing it from a humanistic standpoint."

Bill starts to cry.

The principal continues, "The Lord God Almighty scoffeth at thy futile tears. None of us have the right to question Him. Since you're being argumentative, for this last verse, no ordinary pen will do, William MacDonald Charles. You must show that you really mean it when you confess your sin. For such remission there must be a shedding of blood." He pulls out a syringe, and draws blood from Bill's right wrist without warning. Bill covers his mouth quickly with his left hand to keep from screaming. The principal pours the blood into an old-fashioned fountain pen quill, and hands it to Bill.

It takes almost an hour for Bill to write out those last two sentences, as his head and wrists tremble. His teeth grind. His breath slows to a near stand-still. His bladder is also in pain, and he's afraid he might have an old fashioned accident in his pants. The principal continues to hold his *Bible* in Bill's face, with his fingers on that last verse.

At last, the handwriting torture session is done. The principal says, "All right, you are now free to continue to the next class. However, if you are ever caught with subversive literature again, the consequences will be much more severe, and I will not tell you what they will be. You should be aware there is some subversive literature in the world that is in a special class all its own, that is unforgivable in this world and the next to possess even for a short time. It is called *Class A Categorical Heresy.* It is very rare and hard to come by. It's much easier to buy crystal meth, thank God, although I would never encourage anyone to take illegal drugs. This is one of many reasons that we ended the open internet with the *Published Information Purity Act.* Bottom line, do be very extremely exceedingly careful what books, files, whatever, you read, that's all."

"How are we supposed to know if we have subversive literature? Even the list of banned works, that the prophet John Adramalech Balor wrote, has been blocked on the web behind a credential wall. You can probably see it, but I can't."

"I can't download it, but my boss in the *New White House* can. You don't need to know. Just limit your sources to the, ahem, legitimate outlets. The major retail stores, but not so much the small corner stores which may carry questionable independent art, are very careful to only stock legal material that has been certified not to oppose any of the *Articles of Faith of the Kingdom of God of America*." He points to a large document posted on the wall in a gold frame, which contains the pledge spoken in the morning, and more propaganda of a similar nature. He pulls out a book about trigonometry, and shows the back cover, pointing to a seal on the corner. It is gold-colored, and reads, "*Kingdom of God of America* Approved," with a tiny embossed signature, "John Adramalech Balor, D.D."

The principal continues, "Avoid any kind of counter-culture scene, underground markets, raves, garage and basement shows, whatever its called, as well as trading and borrowing books, games, music and movies with friends, and you won't have to worry about it. This is a very important part of what we call putting the Lord first in your life: be not yoked with unbelievers nor their thoughts nor their emotions. Care, but not too much. Also, consider yourself very luck-, uh, oops, I meant, there for the grace of God, that you were not in possession of something *Class A* such as *Embra-* uh, you don't need to know, it would just break my heart to tell you what I would have to do to you. I did notice that the Mark Twain book in your possession had a counterfeit of the seal of approval, so I will give

16

you some measure of leniency for that. You might have
not known that this was an illegal book. Really, I am
inclined to believe that you did know that the book was
illegal. You hesitated to show it during your random
search."

"That don't prove nothi- oops, I mean, That does
not prove anything."

"You will be free to go home at the normal time
without the usual five hour detention listed in the
Student Code of Conduct for possession of *Class C
Subversive Literature*. Now, may Jesus Christ have
leniency on your soul." He hands Bill a note.

Bill walks out of the office, careful not to express
anything that might be considered suspicious or
disagreeable. He's fortunate that the bathroom is next
door, since he's really gotta go.

Bill is somewhat relieved that he missed a class. It
was the one where they show old videos of the TV
show *Way of the Master*.

In the last class, popcorn and soda are served, and
they show *Hell's Bells The Dangers of Rock 'n Roll*, the
original from 1989 by Erik Hollander and Eric
Holmberg, on the big screen, turned up on 300 watt

tower speakers. What a riot. Nobody took its
cautionary agenda seriously. They really might as well
have screened the Blue Öyster Cult Cowbell sketch
from *Saturday Night Live*. Most just bobbed their
heads to the music samples and amazingly
unintentional slapstick humor. As the scene of the
hospital bed comes up, Jay laughs quietly and whispers
to Bill, "Whitney Houston's *The Greatest Love of All* is
just like death metal? You just can't make this stuff
up."

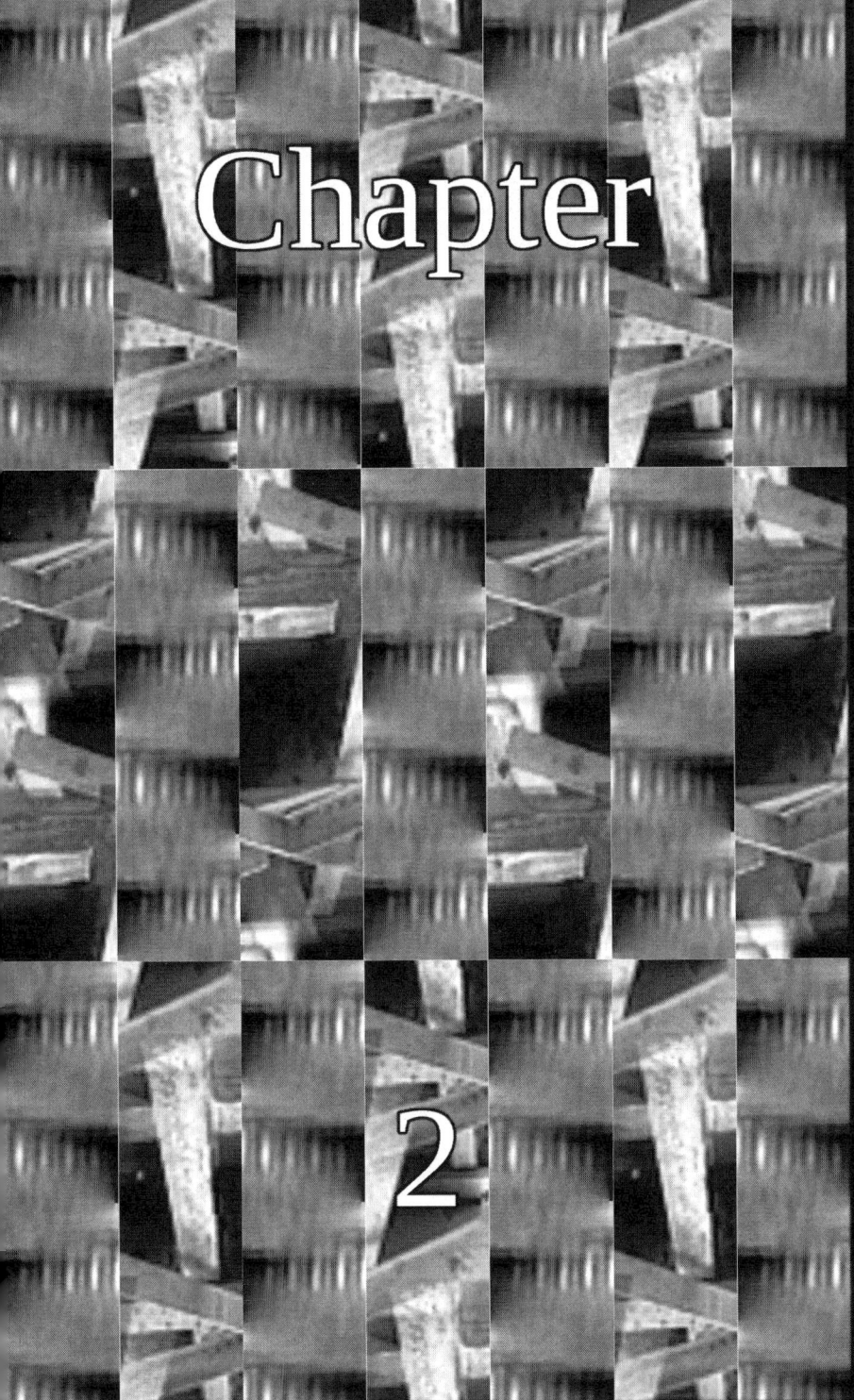

Chapter

2

Bill meets Jay on the way out of the building, and walk onto the streets of Elmore City, Oklahoma. It was once a comically named rural town, but now it has grown to a population of over half a million. The street scene is filled with incredibly boring high-rise apartment buildings that all look exactly the same. There are no trees nor grass anywhere near the sidewalks. If it weren't for the sky, you would think that you were at a gigantic indoor mall. The buildings are so hard to tell apart that you need to read the number on the building to know when you're home, if you would even call it a home.

Jay and Bill reach one of the buildings on Shirley street. The front door to the building is locked, and has a panel with a scanning device. Jay pulls a card out of his pocket, and waves it in front of the scanning device. It beeps, and the door clicks. Jay opens the door, and Bill comes with him into the entry lobby. A computer voice speaks, "Guest detected. No *OCS* chip. Present identification for record."

Jay says, "Your card?"

Bill pulls a card out of his pocket, and waves it before the scanning device.

The voice from the computer says, "Pursuant to the terms of the lease, guest visits are limited to two hours. Please be advised that any extension of the time limit will be charged a fine of one hundred dollars per minute. Please don't forget to have your guests scan their identification upon exit, lest ye be levied the maximum fine of $15,000, of which all residents over the age of 18 shalt be joint and severally liable."

Jay and Bill ride the elevator to floor 71 of the high-rise, and walk down a long hall past seventeen doors. The walls, floor and ceiling are all dull off-white, as well as the doors. All the lighting is very bright florescent, with lots of flicker. There are video cameras everywhere. Jay waves his card at the door. They enter the apartment. It's about a third the size of a what we used to call a cheap motel room. There is no furniture except for three camp cot mattresses. It would be too crowded to hang out in if it had a real bed anyway. They have no large personal belongings, just tiny laptop computers, some clothes and cheap canned food. There is a video camera in the ceiling. In front of the camera is taped a photograph of the room as it is when nobody's there. There is a bar magnet taped to its microphone. Jay says, "I almost never see my mom and dad. Both of them work three jobs, and are still flat broke after the rent. We can only even eat because of the food stamps. And, of course, everyone gives us a hard time about using them."

"They changed what they call them a long time ago."

"I know, but we find the term Supplemental Nutritional Assistance to be even more insulting, not to mention more awkward to say. It almost sounds like it's force-feeding beets or something. And, as you can see, the management control the hell out of us in our own home to boot. We don't keep much, because we are forced to move every few months. My dad's boss is a billionaire, has a very spacious house, and even though he rents, what he pays for that is about half of what our rent costs, and it's all because he has perfect credit. He also owns stock in all the companies that run these apartment buildings. I fear the day when I turn 18, when I will be forced to sign all those contracts that my parents already do. I can't count the times I saw my mom break down and cry, and gnash her teeth in terror, her face turning hot white, while the building management agents smirk at her without a hint of any kind of empathy or remorse. They write these contracts in such a way that no matter how careful you are, some kind of accidental violation of the contract is outright inevitable; it's total walking-on-eggshells. Fair as baseball, one hit and caught ball and you're out. Pushed around from one rental company to another, they go through this process over and over and over again. And, the more evictions on the credit report, the more they hike up the prices. No, we never got behind on rent, it's always for them nitpicking over the rules. I think I'd rather go on the run from the civilized world, or even die than have to live like that. I'm not looking forward to high school graduation at all. One time an ambulance had to be called when my mom had a heart attack during the lease signing ritual. The doctor signed the lease for her using a temporary incapacity power of attorney. Then, the management sent her a letter. The letter said, 'Please be advised that you will be held accountable as if you had signed the contract willingly, in wholehearted agreement.' Wholehearted agreement? Interesting choice of words, as those who write these forms don't seem to have even half a heart.

24

Everyone knows, people are being forced to sign these
things. They didn't really need to change contract law
that much when we converted to a monarchy, as there
had already been plenty of coercion by collusion in
what was called the free market era. My parents have
been sued for the rest of the year's rent after getting
kicked out four times, and as a result went through two
bankruptcies. And, of course, the more bad stuff that's
on the credit report, the more nitpicky they get when
we're trying to get another place. They bring up every
false charge that all the past landlords wrote about us as
if their words were the effing Gospel for Chri-, uh, I
mean for crying out loud. Eventually, we'll have no
choice but to just let them lock us up. I can't imagine
how the chattel slavery of the pre-Civil-War era could
have been much worse than this. At least those slaves
weren't sent filling out applications to beg for a new
slave-owner to accept them every few months under
deadline pressures. When my mom and dad try to seek
a lawyer for help with our rights, they always change
the subject to 'rights and responsibilities.' It's quite
clear that the lawyers work for them, not us, but they
are willing to take our money and give us patronizing

education. Real advocacy for the downtrodden does
not seem to exist in the lawyer business anymore.

Bill knows that Jay is often making trouble, and
could just be mouthing off. However, many of the very
same things are starting to happen to his own family,
and it is gradually getting worse.

Jay is cooking some toast in the toaster, and
watching it closely. "I have to be very careful, the
smoke detector doesn't just beep, and there's no stop
button. The computer force-evacuates the whole
building every time someone burns their toast. And,
you better do exactly what you're supposed to, or else.
It goes on record with the lease enforcement
department if they catch you saving any of your own
personal belongings. Yes, they actually have two full
time employees with *"Lease Enforcement Specialist"* as
their job title, and they are offered overtime pay
generously. Nobody who lives here dares to look them
in the eye for any reason. Most turn off the radio or TV
and hide in the bathroom when the sound of their high
heels is heard as they patrol the halls. About the only
thing missing is the Korean army's high-kicking march
style. People have learned to be extremely cautious,

but a big alarm and follow-up interrogation happens about once a week. How's your family's place?"

"Pretty much the same thing. It's on Arrowhead Drive, but if you didn't check the number and street name you would not be able to tell our buildings apart, inside or out. Not much of a home, when you just can't wait to get out of it. Only legal place to sleep, shower and cook a meal, otherwise we really live on the streets. That's what we get for nearly my parents' entire income. We barely have enough to put six quarters in the shower each time we use it, and it only runs for forty seconds. It works like a self-service car wash bay. My dad can only afford to take a shower twice a week on this machine, and has to hide this fact from his bosses. My mom and dad would say, at least the work bosses are not as bossy as the landlords. When it rains, Dad would take a walk with his shirt off just to get some free body cleaning from nature's gift, although he has to watch out for the bugs, especially the flying scorpions. He gets really shaky from the fear when he gets home on the third day since his last shower. Mom doesn't have that option. She gets a bad rash if she doesn't wash at least every two days."

Jay and Bill pack some suitcases. Jay says, "Shh," waves his hand between the camera and decoy picture while he pulls the picture and magnet off of the camera, and hides them in his backpack.

They leave the building, waving their cards to the computer to report their exit. As they are walking, Bill says, "Wh-"

Jay cuts in, "Shh. Wait till we're on the outskirts of town."

Two hours walking west on Route 29, Jay says, "We're almost there. What a shame that my parents pay most of their wages, for not only a miserable excuse for a home, but one we literally avoid as much as possible. That's one of the reasons I go to sleep-over parties so much. By the way, the magnet jams the microphone so they can't hear us talking."

"I know. We're doing the same thing, although they don't know about the camera trick. I hope not to ever be in their shoes. I'm also seriously considering just going on the run when I come of age. If I try to do everything right, and will be treated like a criminal anyway for some slight inevitable imperfection, what's the point?"

"If there is any place to run left in the whole world, that is. By the way, this party will be quite historic. Rick is about to reveal his top secret invention."

"I can't wait to see it."

They arrive at an abandoned motel. Japanese knotweed is eating away at its walls. Beetles, mice, ants and rats scurry about the foundation. There are no cars near the building. The windows are all boarded up. It is quiet. Jay says, "Here's the place."

"Nobody's home but the rats and the beetles?"

"Only looks that way. We keep it very discreet. Come in quickly!"

Chapter

3

Bill and Jay enter the abandoned motel. They open their suitcases and change their clothes. Bill puts on a blue polyester vented shirt with a reflective laser-etched pattern, and shiny thin navy blue nylon jogging pants. Jay has a similar shirt that's green, and thin wind pants in a lighter shade of blue that have a small rip on the front side, about two inches below the seam between the legs, showing part of his bright shiny white sport-compression underwear. Depending on what mood you're in, it's either super-cute or disgusting. A white key-chain-lanyard strap hangs out of Jay's pants' pocket, dangling about two feet down the side of his leg. It swings forward and backward as Jay walks, and the pants make a swishing sound as the legs move.

Bill says, "We wouldn't get caught dead wearing something like that in school."

Jay whips Bill gently on the side of his leg using the lanyard strap. Bill is tickled and giggles a bit.

Jay says, "Hey, enjoy yourself while you can. The good old days." Jay pulls out some pictures taken in high school from the 1990s and early 2000s. "This was my dad. In his day, the public high school kids were this casual and sexy all the time, and nobody cared."

He pulls a sheet of button candy out of the side of his briefs opposite to the little rip. He plucks two pieces off the paper, then puts the sheet in his right pocket. "We still had to be discreet about this stuff, though." He eats one of the candy pieces.

"Why, just one tiny piece of candy?"

"LSD mixed with a little MDMA." He holds out the other piece.

Bill somehow just doesn't want to do any drugs tonight, but wants to play the part and fit in. He's more interested in the invention, and wants to remember it well. He takes the piece of candy. He hides it in his hand, pretends to put it in his mouth, then puts it in his pocket. Bill sits down on a lounge chair.

A young man wearing knee-length purple shorts with a turquoise image of a sea shell on them, and a white mesh shirt, is setting up sound equipment on the other end of the room. He plugs an amplifier, a disco ball, and a laser projector into a portable power supply. Classic disco music begins to play softly, and the walls glow with colors.

A door opens. A girl walks into the room. She looks about 15, has dark black hair in a pony tail and glassy blue eyes. She is wearing very tight-fitting jog pants, almost like yoga leggings but just a little bit thicker, glossy indigo with reflective lines in a laser diagonal pattern. Her shirt looks like a classic tye-dye of orange and blue, but it's glossy mesh polyester. Over it is a tight-fitting bright blue shiny thin nylon hoodie jacket, almost clear as glass, with vent flaps on the back, and her shirt is seen through it. Bill sees her for a split second, then looks to the side. Jay, still standing, turns sideways, and lifts his right leg and puts it on a footstool. His right leg faces away from the seat, and toward the door that the girl walked in.

The girl smiles and runs toward Jay. She runs into him, touching the front of her jog tights to the side of his raised leg. She pushes Jay onto the couch by lifting the left side of his bottom, and taunts, "Jay-Sin."

Jay's real name is James. He had been Bill's closest friend since first grade. He usually went by the nickname Jay. Around the age of 14 some started calling him Jay-Sin, as he had become quite a flirt. Jay had changed from his innocence quickly, in a way that might remind you of an animal that you're not supposed to ever let eat after dark. Since his last name is Eal, he could just as well have been nicknamed St. Eal. He steals. His suitcase is packed with bottles of beer and liquor that he, as he would boast, "downloaded from the grocery store, no ID necessary."

Bill has mixed feelings about the sight in front of him. It's ticklishly cute to watch. He's also a bit uneasy. He's looking down and to the side, only sneaking an occasional quick glance at what is right in front of him.

Jay looks at Bill, and says, "Hey Billy, enjoy yourself. This is my girlbuddy Katy." Jay picks up the girl, and throws her onto Bill. The front-center of Katy's tight pants fall right onto Bill's lap. The white draw-strings on Katy's jog pants rub across Bill's, tickling a sensitive organ. Katy rubs the side of her legs, laughs, and gets up. Bill's heart begins to race with both arousal and unease. He sees her smooth-skinned face and her bouncy legs. She opens up her pony tail, and lets her hair flow around. She turns dance-like in a circle, so Bill sees her from all sides. With what she's wearing, her slender bottom is even more provocative to Bill than if it were naked. Almost involuntarily, he thinks of cuddling her, and playing with her pants and jacket, but can't really bring himself to do it. After all, she is Jay's girlbuddy. Bill thought, "Why did he throw her on me like that?"

Jay says, "And that's Billy, Katy."

The sound system is turned up a bit. The MC announces, "Welcome to our *Information Freedom Rave*. We do have some long-awaited and awesome news to tell tonight, but first we'll play some grooves to get the party started." Cheers are heard echoing through the many rooms of the motel.

Jay grabs Katy and they front-to-front freak-dance to the classic disco music. The aroma of cheap beer and marijuana smoke starts to fill the whole building.

Bill gets up from the couch, and starts to walk toward a door. He's thinking about looking around to see what's going on in the other rooms.

As Bill reaches the door, he feels arms touch his shoulders. He is grabbed and turned around. Katy throws him back to Jay. Bill's shoes slide across the floor, which is slippery damp from spilled beer. Katy smiles and giggles as Bill's body crashes into hers. Jay walks toward them. Bill is caught between Katy and Jay for a few seconds, then the song ends. Bill is quite relieved, yet acts like he likes it all. Katy smiles, winks, and shakes Bill's hands. They sit down on the couch. Katy sits in the middle of the couch, almost on Bill, nearly pinning him to the corner. Jay sits down on the other corner.

The MC speaks, "Welcome to our Information Freedom Rave! Tonight we have a truly exciting announcement! We have found the ultimate solution to break through the censored Internet. Our testing has proven that it works. We have invented..." A drum roll is heard. "*The Bamboo Router.* How did we come up with this name? We thought of it when reflecting on the how and why bamboo is often hard to get rid of. This technology uses *macroscale quantum particle entanglement* to communicate information between any points instantly. It makes both wire communication and radio signals obsolete. It's also impossible to eavesdrop on. *Macroscale quantum particle entanglement* communication is like a wormhole. There is not even a trace in the air of the signal being sent. Nothing can stop it. The *Ministry* goons can try, but good luck to them, Not! It does not need anything to pass through, not even space. It goes from one point to the other as if no distance existed. Even the speed of light has been conquered for information transmission. This is an even greater breakthrough than restoring the good old days of the open internet. No more phone and cable bills, and no limit to the bandwidth it can carry. It is truly peer-to-peer and self sufficient. Now I know that most of you won't understand most of the nerd-talk that I just explained, so I'll put it in simpler terms. We've brought the open internet back for free and much more!" Applause and cheers are heard throughout the building. "You will all be free to take one of these devices home with you. We have formed a gift economy after all." More music is cued up.

Bill understands much of what's being talked about here. He did study *quantum physics,* for he loves this stuff. However, he knows that we've never been able to use this particle entanglement phenomenon in a useful way, because of what they call collapse by observation. Bill thinks, "Did someone find a way around it? If this is true, it could mean that time machines are next."

Bill sneaks away from Jay and Katy and goes to another room, where he meets the MC Rick, and an elderly woman. She is dressed in bell bottom jeans and matching denim shirt. She says, "Hello, I'm Melissa. I can see that you're among the wiser kind."

"William MacDonald Charles, you can call me Billy or even Billy the Square for all I care." Bill's not quite a square, he had done drugs, but is trying to quit.

Melissa whispers, "I hate drugs too, but I hide it to try and fit in. I'm here for Rick's project. I have quite an important use for it, so I hope and pray it works. Now, to be honest, it will mostly be used for shady activities, selling drugs, pirating music, movies, books and video games, and probably identity theft and terrorism too. However, I hope that it will carry some important truth that I wish to expose to the world."

Bill immediately thinks of the missing text on the Norman Rockwell artwork. He silently reflects, "Just how much are they hiding from us?"

Rick says, "We nerds always faced a social catch-22. I heard you've got some serious goods?"

"Oh yea. As serious as it gets."

"Our internet-reborn is growing fast! The *Bamboo Routers* have only been out at the rave parties for five minutes, and they already restored over half of the old internet's vast storehouse of information that was lost, from pirate backups people kept. About half of the lost videos from *YouTube* are back, most of *Wikipedia,* and the entire collection of *Project Gutenberg.* I can't believe all this happened in just five minutes! It almost makes Biblical miracles seem scientific, doesn't it?"

"Biblical, in more sense than one. We will still have quite a battle on our hands, especially if John Adramalech Balor finds out. What I brought to upload tonight is as Biblical as it gets, literally."

"Hence one of our favorite slogans in our *Information Freedom Raves*: *Save Freedom of Worship. Fuck John Adramalech Balor!"*

"Feel sorry for the woman that has to."

Rick falls on the floor and laughs hard. He gets up, "Now that's a good one, Melissa. Sympathy for the Whore of Babylon!"

"It's great that we've got all that done so quickly." Melissa takes a *Bamboo Router* and hooks it up to her laptop and starts the web browser. "Just like it used to be, and hopefully better?" She loads up John Adramalech Balor's list of banned works, and says, "Lets explore some of the things that they don't want us to have, and why. As shown in this document, the *Published Information Purity Act* defines four distinct classes of *Subversive Literature.* The same law applies to movies, music and games. *Class D* is described as a potential risk to Christian Orthodoxy, yet still may be enjoyed responsibly with extreme caution. You gotta be 21 to buy it. *Class C* is called *Antiauthoritarian,* and carries a flexible penalty depending on the details of circumstances on a case-by-case basis. *Class B* is called *Overtone Heresy,* with similar penalties to *Class C. Class A* is called *Categorical Heresy,* and it is unforgivable to possess. In John Adramalech Balor's own words, you will get your head chopped off and go to Hell. I have noticed a shocking fact. Many of the banned works are Christian, and some that weren't banned were modified using a bait-and-switch technique. There also seems to be no consistency to the classing. I'll give a few examples among thousands on the list."

Melissa continues, "Some of Billy Graham's books written close to the end of his life have a few paragraphs taken out of them. Katherine Kuhlman, Max Lucado, T.D. Jakes, Joel Osteen, and many others

have also been heavily edited. Several songs by
Michael W. Smith, Amy Grant and Gary Chapman had
a few verses of their lyrics taken out of them.
According to John Adramalech Balor's notes, 'I
regarded these three songwriters as new-age-
infiltrators, but couldn't bring myself to ban their
music. I did the next best thing, in a way that nobody
noticed the censorship.' People gave up their old
books, records, tapes, CDs and DVDs when offered
new-and-improved remastered copies in exchange for
free, without being told that parts were taken out of the
new copies. Of course, everyone's Spotify, iTunes, etc.
got updated quietly. I remember when John
Adramalech Balor liked Sean Hannity, but, he says, the
bridge was burned when the movie *Let There Be Light*
came out. It's marked *Class B* for hints of *implied
universal salvation*. In the details column, Balor wrote,
'How dare he betray us, what sheer audacity to make a
character that dies while on tour to preach atheism, yet
still gets into heaven, then lives to tell the tale?'
Among other notable works on the *Class A* list, of
which there are thousands more, *Embraced by the
Light* by Betty Eadie, *The Shack* by William Paul

Young, *Love Wins* by Robert Bell, The TV Shows *Touched by an Angel*, *Ghost Whisperer*, and *Supernatural*. He also banned George MacDonald's *The Hope of the Gospel*, a-"

Bill cuts in, "WHAT? We get arrested and have our heads chopped off for having a book called *The Hope of the Gospel*?"

"No joke. Most of George MacDonald's books are banned, except for a few of the cute children's stories that don't say too much. By the way, REM's *Losing My Religion* is still on the radio. Balor doesn't seem to mind AC/DC's *Highway to Hell* being on the radio all the time. Slayer and Venom are class D, which you can buy if you are 21. Somehow this so-called Christian regime doesn't mind if you listen to *Burn the Cross* by Coven, provided you can get someone 21 to buy it for you! The Rolling Stones? Most of it is Class D. John Adramalech Balor actually liked one particular song, that hymn about not always getting what you want. Yep, he made it an official hymn. Nearly all the music by The Moody Blues, Glade Swope, and Kansas, is banned, most of it class B and some of it class A. *Bridge to Terabithia* is also banned, class B.

Somehow Balor has no problem with any of the *Friday the Thirteenth* and *Nightmare on Elm Street* movies. Oh, you won't believe this, John Adramalech Balor changed them to a G rating because he believes," she points to the screen, "almost as enlightening as the *A Thief in the Night* series, these films are an excellent influence, as they promote the true gospel. You can still buy *Led Zeppelin Four* without being 21, but now it comes with the *Hells Bells Dangers of Rock 'n Roll* DVD. I guess they want to make sure everyone knows that you have to play the record backwards."

While opening up a box on the floor carefully, Melissa says, "Now speaking of the quest to find that tool shed by the brook where the devil keeps his pitchfork, wait till you see what I've got to show you next. You're not gonna believe it 'till you see it. It's more Biblical than an army of giant marshmallowmen."

Chapter

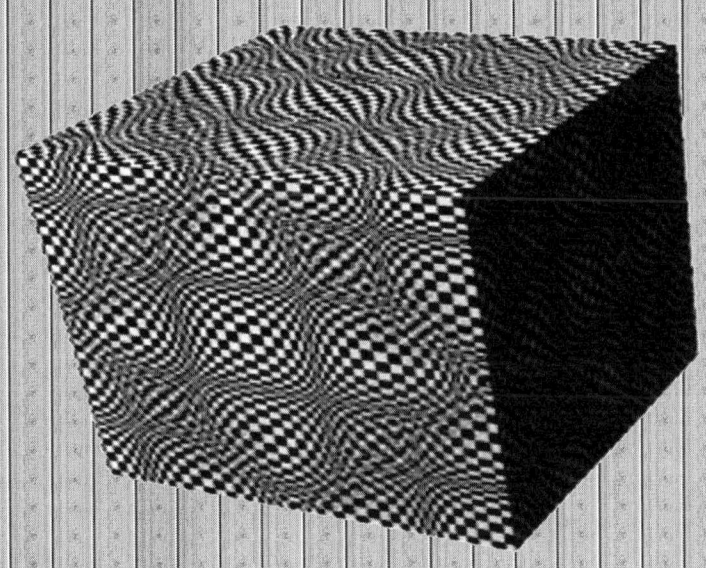

4

Melissa pulls out a note from a cardboard box on the floor and begins to read, "I have placed this *King James Bible* in this specially designed box, that blocks the gamma waves produced by the Mandela Effect Machine. Do not expose it for more than a few minutes. I don't know how long it's safe to expose it, so keep it enclosed in this box as much as possible. I have scanned a backup copy to a USB flash drive, but still be careful. When the effect takes place, compare carefully."

Bill says, "What the heck is a Mandela Effect Machine?"

Melissa says, "I don't know, but I hope to find out. Someone wouldn't pack a Bible in a science experiment like this for no reason." She pulls a book out of her purse. "See this *King James Bible* just purchased from the store?"

"What about it?"

Melissa reads the same passage that Bill was forced to copy out in detention, ending with "No one talketh back at the Lord God and live. Thy daughter be vexed with a devil indeed, for she belongs to him. She will surely be cast into Hell forever, along with you likewise unless ye repent of your rebellion."

Melissa opens the metal box, pulls a Bible out of it, and turns it to the same verse, shows it and says, "Now this one reads: O woman, great is thy faith: be it unto thee even as thou wilt. And her daughter was made whole from that very hour." She quickly places this Bible back in the metal box, and closes it.

"Why the hurry?"

"Hopefully you won't see the reason for it." She turns the store-bought Bible to *Matthew* 17, "And after six days Jesus taketh Peter, James, and John his brother, and bringeth them up into an high mountain apart, And was transfigured before them: and his face did shine as the sun, and his raiment was white as the light. And, behold, there appeared unto them Moses and Elias."

Melissa pulls the Bible from the metal box, and shows the same verse. There are three more words in the third verse, "talking with him." She quickly puts it back in the metal box and closes it.

Melissa turns the store-bought Bible to *First John* Chapter *2*, "If we sin, we have an advocate with the Father, Jesus Christ the righteous: And He is the propitiation for our sins, yet not for the sins of the whole world."

The Bible in the box reads, "My little children, these things write I unto you, that ye sin not. And if any man sin, we have an advocate with the Father, Jesus Christ the righteous: And He is the propitiation for our sins, and not for ours only, but also the sins of the whole world."

Bill is already in enough shock already at what he sees. Zap! The words in the Bible from the box, like magic, change instantly to match what was in the store-bought Bible the instant Melissa finished saying, "whole world." Melissa says, "Oh, no. At least you saw it. I pray that the electronic file is good." She loads the USB stick into the laptop, "Oh, thank God. Let's continue."

The store-bought Bible in *First Peter 4:6* says, "For for this cause the gospel is not preached to them that are dead, for they can only receive God into their spirit while they live as men in the flesh, but are judged forever once in the spirit."

The backup file says, "For for this cause was the gospel preached also to them that are dead, that they might be judged according to men in the flesh, but live according to God in the spirit."

Melissa turns the store-bought to *Matthew 4:24* and says, "Very small difference, you have to look very closely to notice." "And his fame went throughout all Syria: and they brought unto him some sick people that were taken with divers diseases and torments, and those which were possessed with devils, and those which were lunatick, and those that had the palsy; and he healed them."

The backup reads, "And his fame went throughout all Syria: and they brought unto him all sick people that were taken with divers diseases and torments, and those which were possessed with devils, and those which were lunatick, and those that had the palsy; and he healed them."

The store-bought Bible in *Matthew 10:8* says, "Heal the sick, cleanse the lepers, cast out devils: freely ye have received, freely give."

The backup reads, "Heal the sick, cleanse the lepers, raise the dead, cast out devils: freely ye have received, freely give."

Romans 6:23 in the store-bought Bible says, "For the wages of sin is eternal torment, but the gift of God is eternal life for those who are in Jesus Christ our Lord."

The backup reads, "For the wages of sin is death; but the gift of God is eternal life through Jesus Christ our Lord."

John 1:1-9 in the store-bought Bible says, "In the beginning was the Word, and the Word was with God, and the Word was God. The same was in the beginning with God. All things were made by Him; yet not all things were made with Him. In Him was life; and the life was the light of some men. And the light passeth by the darkness; for the darkness comprehended it not. There was a man sent from God, whose name was John. The same came for a witness, to bear witness of the Light, that some men through him might believe. He was not that Light, but was sent to bear witness of that Light. That was the true Light, which may lighteth some men that cometh into the world. "

The backup reads, "In the beginning was the Word, and the Word was with God, and the Word was God. The same was in the beginning with God. All things were made by Him; and without Him was not any thing made that was made. In Him was life; and the life was the light of men. And the light shineth in darkness; and the darkness comprehended it not. There was a man sent from God, whose name was John. The same came for a witness, to bear witness of the Light, that all men through him might believe. He was not that Light, but was sent to bear witness of that Light. That was the true Light, which lighteth every man that cometh into the world. "

John 1:29 from the store Bible reads, "The next day John seeth Jesus coming unto him, and saith, Behold the Lamb of God, which taketh some men away from the sins of the world."

The backup, "The next day John seeth Jesus coming unto him, and saith, Behold the Lamb of God, which taketh away the sin of the world."

John 4:41-42 from store-bought reads, "And many more believed because of his own word; And said unto the woman, Now we believe, not because of thy saying: for we have heard him ourselves, and know that this is indeed the Christ, our personal Savior, and ours alone."

The backup, "And many more believed because of his own word; And said unto the woman, Now we believe, not because of thy saying: for we have heard him ourselves, and know that this is indeed the Christ, the Savior of the world."

John 4:49-53 in store-bought reads, "The nobleman saith unto him, Sir, come down ere my child die. Jesus saith unto him, Go away; unless he believe, thy son perish. And the man believed the word that Jesus had spoken unto him, and he went away sorrowful. Then inquired he of them the hour when the child expired. And they said unto him, Yesterday at the seventh hour the breath of life left him. So the father knew that it was at the same hour, in the which Jesus said unto him, Unless he believe, thy son perish: yet himself believed, and the rest of his house."

The backup, "The nobleman saith unto him, Sir, come down ere my child die. Jesus saith unto him, Go thy way; thy son liveth. And the man believed the word that Jesus had spoken unto him, and he went his way. Then inquired he of them the hour when he began to amend. And they said unto him, Yesterday at the seventh hour the fever left him. So the father knew that it was at the same hour, in the which Jesus said unto him, Thy son liveth: and himself believed, and his whole house."

John 21:25 in store-bought reads, "And these are all of the things which Jesus did, to wit, I have written every one, yet in the world will be written many books that should not be written. Amen."

The backup says, "And there are also many other things which Jesus did, the which, if they should be written every one, I suppose that even the world itself could not contain the books that should be written. Amen."

Acts 5:16 in store-bought, "There came also a multitude out of the cities round about unto Jerusalem, bringing sick folks, and them which were vexed with unclean spirits: and a few were healed."

The backup, "There came also a multitude out of the cities round about unto Jerusalem, bringing sick folks, and them which were vexed with unclean spirits: and they were healed every one."

Acts 10:36-38 in store-bought, "The word which God sent unto the children of Israel, preaching to accept Jesus Christ: for He is not Lord of all :(That word, I say, ye know, which was published throughout all Judea, and began from Galilee, after the baptism which John preached; How God anointed Jesus of Nazareth with the Holy Ghost and with power: who went about doing good, and healing some that were oppressed of the devil; for God was with him."

Backup, "The word which God sent unto the children of Israel, preaching peace by Jesus Christ: (he is Lord of all:) That word, I say, ye know, which was published throughout all Judea, and began from Galilee, after the baptism which John preached; How God anointed Jesus of Nazareth with the Holy Ghost and with power: who went about doing good, and healing all that were oppressed of the devil; for God was with him."

Romans 5:18 in the store-bought, "By the offense of one judgment came upon all men to condemnation; even so by the righteousness of one the free gift came upon some men unto justification of life."

The backup, "Therefore as by the offense of one judgment came upon all men to condemnation; even so by the righteousness of one the free gift came upon all men unto justification of life."

Melissa turns the store-bought to *Romans 6:7*, "Now this one is really shocking." "For he that is dead in his sins is irredeemably and forever lost."

The backup, "For he that is dead is freed from sin."

Bill is so surprised that he almost falls out of his chair.

Melissa says, "Here's another good one. *Romans 9:22*." From store-bought, "God, willing to shew his wrath, and to make his power known, endured with much longsuffering the vessels of wrath fitted to destruction."

Backup, "What if God, willing to shew his wrath, and to make his power known, endured with much longsuffering the vessels of wrath fitted to destruction."

Bill flinches again, "What if? In the Bible? Really? You know they send us to detention in school just for mentioning that phrase?"

"Yes, and of course that's not the only reason for deleting it. The clock reads 11:25 PM. How about that? *11:25*." "For I would not, brethren, that ye should be ignorant of this mystery, lest ye should be wise in your own conceits; that blindness in part is happened to Israel, until a portion of the Gentiles be come in."

Backup, "For I would not, brethren, that ye should be ignorant of this mystery, lest ye should be wise in your own conceits; that blindness in part is happened to

Israel, until the fullness of the Gentiles be come in."

"Now starting with verse *30*," "For as ye in times past have not believed God, yet have now obtained mercy through your belief: Even so have these also now not believed, they will not all obtain mercy. For God hath concluded them all in unbelief. He may have mercy upon some."

Backup, "For as ye in times past have not believed God, yet have now obtained mercy through their unbelief: Even so have these also now not believed, that through your mercy they also may obtain mercy. For God hath concluded them all in unbelief, that he might have mercy upon all."

Matthew 7:1 in store-bought, "Judge not, except that thou shalt judge by the Word of God."

Backup, "Judge not, that ye be not judged."

First John 4:7-8 in store-bought, "God is love. However, love is not God."

Backup, "Beloved, let us love one another: for love is of God; and every one that loveth is born of God, and knoweth God. He that loveth not knoweth not God; for God is love."

Verses *17-19* in store-bought, "Herein is our fear of

God made perfect, that we may have leniency in the day of judgment: because as he is, we are not, nor ever can be. We must fear Him, for He will torment. He might loveth us, if we first love Him."

Backup, "Herein is our love made perfect, that we may have boldness in the day of judgment: because as he is, so are we in this world. There is no fear in love; but perfect love casteth out fear: because fear hath torment. He that feareth is not made perfect in love. We love him, because he first loved us."

First Corinthians 5:3-5 in store-bought, "For verily, concerning him that hath so done this deed, is judged already, In the name of our Lord Jesus Christ, when ye are gathered together, and my spirit, with the power of our Lord Jesus Christ, To deliver such an one unto Satan for the destruction of body and soul in Hell in the day of the Lord Jesus."

Backup, "For I verily, as absent in body, but present in spirit, have judged already, as though I were present, concerning him that hath so done this deed, In the name of our Lord Jesus Christ, when ye are gathered together, and my spirit, with the power of our Lord Jesus Christ, To deliver such an one unto Satan for the destruction of the flesh, that the spirit may be saved in the day of the Lord Jesus."

Bill says, "A spirit being saved in the beyond, after being judged and delivered to Satan? They'd hang us for Class A New Age Heresy for even suggesting something like that. They're always telling us that there ain't no second chances on the other side of the grave, you know."

"This is the original King James, or at least it was. This particular copy of the Bible has been in my family for seven generations, and now it just got ruined. However, I realize that an even greater tragedy was averted just in the nick of time. I guess that someone really did build a machine to modify all the Bibles in the world, but who did it and how? And why? Talk about a Famine for the Hearing of the Word! I just put the backup on our new internet. Bombshell. I'm not gonna let them get away with this, come hell or high water."

Chapter

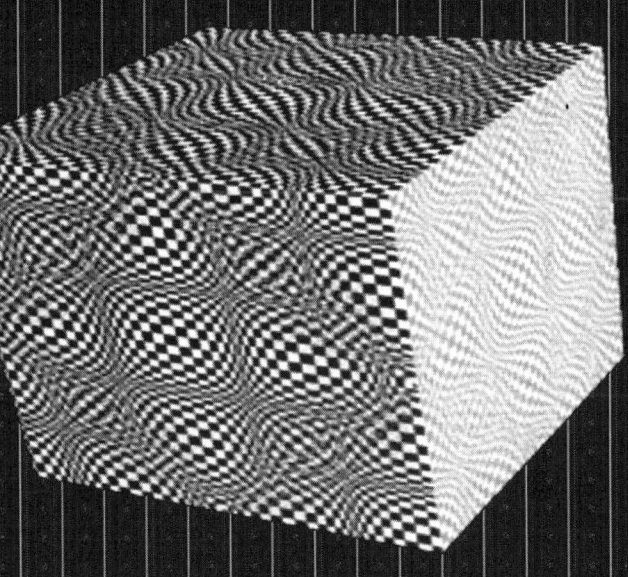

5

Melissa continues, "Let's continue with *First Corinthians 12:6.*" "And there are diversities of operations, but it is the same God which worketh all in us."

Backup, "And there are diversities of operations, but it is the same God which worketh all in all."

Bill says, "All in all? Really? One time I wrote in my homework essay about *The Pilgrim's Progress*, 'All in all, I found it difficult to follow,' and I was carted off to detention so quickly that the way they treated me, I might as well have written the word 'fuck' into my book report."

"Oh no, it's not the only one."

First Corinthians 15:22-28 in store-bought, "For as in Adam all die, even so in Christ shall some be made alive. But each of these in his own order: Christ the first-fruits; afterward they that are Christ's at his coming. Then cometh the end, when he shall have delivered up the kingdom to God, even the Father; when he shall have rule and authority and power. For he must reign, till he hath put all enemies under his feet. The end of a man's opportunity to find redemption for his spirit is death. For Christ hath put all things under his feet. But when he saith all things are put under him, it is manifest that he is excepted, which did put all things under him. And when all things shall be subdued unto him, then shall the Son also himself be subject unto him that put all things under him. God is God."

Backup, "For as in Adam all die, even so in Christ shall all be made alive. But every man in his own order: Christ the first-fruits; afterward they that are Christ's at his coming. Then cometh the end, when he shall have delivered up the kingdom to God, even the Father; when he shall have put down all rule and all authority and power. For he must reign, till he hath put all enemies under his feet. The last enemy that shall be destroyed is death. For he hath put all things under his feet. But when he saith all things are put under him, it is manifest that he is excepted, which did put all things under him. And when all things shall be subdued unto him, then shall the Son also himself be subject unto him that put all things under him, that God may be all in all."

"You realize, if one of us were caught saying 'that God may be all in all', they'd try and convict for blasphemy as quickly as if we were to scream 'God is the Devil?'"

"We have been brainwashed to call a lot of good evil and call a lot of evil good. Yea, it's common knowledge that John Adramalech Balor always hated the phrase 'all in all.' He claims that in the very sound of that phrase is the very essence of the devil, so of course, he banned the Earth Wind and Fire album. I'm not surprised that he whacked it from the Bible at all. For good measure, the next verse, *29*." "Else what shall they do which are baptized for their salvation? Why are they then baptized for their salvation?"

Backup, "Else what shall they do which are baptized for the dead, if the dead rise not at all? why are they then baptized for the dead?"

Melissa comments, "Yea, John Adramalech Balor often warns about the danger of honoring the dead too much. He would say he's not quite from Westboro Kansas, but, ... Now *Second Corinthians 3:6*." "Who also hath made us able ministers of the new testament; of the letter and of the spirit: for the letter with the spirit giveth life."

Backup, "Who also hath made us able ministers of

the new testament; not of the letter, but of the spirit: for the letter killeth, but the spirit giveth life."

Second Corinthians 5:17-19, "Therefore if any man be in Christ, he is a saved sinner: old things are passed away, yet some things are become new. Not all things are of God, yet He hath reconciled us to himself by Jesus Christ, and hath given to us the ministry of reconciliation; To wit, that God was in Christ, reconciling just us unto Himself, not imputing our trespasses unto us; and hath committed unto us alone the word of reconciliation."

Backup, "Therefore if any man be in Christ, he is a new creature: old things are passed away; behold, all things are become new. And all things are of God, who hath reconciled us to himself by Jesus Christ, and hath given to us the ministry of reconciliation; To wit, that God was in Christ, reconciling the world unto himself, not imputing their trespasses unto them; and hath committed unto us the word of reconciliation."

Store-bought *Galatians 3:24-25*, "Wherefore the law was our schoolmaster to bring us unto Christ, that we might be justified by faith. That faith is come; nevertheless, we are yet under the schoolmaster."

Backup, "Wherefore the law was our schoolmaster to bring us unto Christ, that we might be justified by faith. But after that faith is come, we are no longer under a schoolmaster."

Galatians 5:1, "Stand fast therefore in the obedience wherewith Christ hath made us free from sin, and be entangled with the yoke of His bondage."

Backup, "Stand fast therefore in the liberty wherewith Christ hath made us free, and be not entangled again with the yoke of bondage."

Ephesians 2:15, "Having exempted some from the enmity, in the flesh, even abolished some of the law of commandments contained in ordinances; for to bring some to himself, so making peace; And that he might reconcile some unto God in one body by the cross, having appeased the enmity thereby."

Backup, "Having abolished in his flesh the enmity, even the law of commandments contained in ordinances; for to make in himself of twain one new man, so making peace; And that he might reconcile both unto God in one body by the cross, having slain the enmity thereby."

Ephesians 3:17-19, "That Christ may dwell in your

hearts by faith; that ye, being rooted and grounded in fear, May be able to comprehend with all saints the limited atonement; the breadth, and length, and depth, and height; And to know that we must have love for Christ, by our knowledge, that ye might be filled with the fear of God."

Backup, "That Christ may dwell in your hearts by faith; that ye, being rooted and grounded in love, May be able to comprehend with all saints what is the breadth, and length, and depth, and height; And to know the love of Christ, which passeth knowledge, that ye might be filled with all the fullness of God."

Ephesians 4:9-10, "Now that he ascended, what is it but that he also descended first into some of the earth? He that descended is the same also that ascended up far above all heavens, that he might fill some things."

Backup, "Now that he ascended, what is it but that he also descended first into the lower parts of the earth? He that descended is the same also that ascended up far above all heavens, that he might fill all things."

Colossians 1:16-20, "For by him were all things created, that are in heaven, and that are in earth, visible and invisible, whether they be thrones, or dominions, or principalities, or powers: all things were created by him, and some for him: And was before all things, and by him some things consist. And he is the head of the body, the church: who is the beginning, the firstborn from the living; that in some things he might have the preeminence. For it pleased the Father that in him should a portion dwell; And, having made selection through the blood of his cross, by him to reconcile some things unto himself; by him, I say, whether they be things in earth, or things in heaven."

Backup, "For by him were all things created, that are in heaven, and that are in earth, visible and invisible, whether they be thrones, or dominions, or principalities, or powers: all things were created by him, and for him: And he is before all things, and by him all things consist. And he is the head of the body, the church: who is the beginning, the firstborn from the dead; that in all things he might have the preeminence. For it pleased the Father that in him should all fullness dwell; And, having made peace through the blood of his cross, by him to reconcile all things unto himself; by him, I say, whether they be things in earth, or things in heaven."

Colossians 3:15, "And let the terror of God rule in your hearts, to the which also ye are called in one body; be ye thankful ye not be among them that perish."

Backup, "And let the peace of God rule in your hearts, to the which also ye are called in one body; and be ye thankful."

Colossians 3:25, "But he that is not one of us, but one of them that perish, shall receive for the wrong which he hath done."

Backup, "But he that doeth wrong shall receive for the wrong which he hath done: and there is no respect of persons."

First Timothy 1:20, "Of whom is Hymenaeus and Alexander; whom I have delivered unto Satan, that they be tormented forever."

Backup, "Of whom is Hymenaeus and Alexander; whom I have delivered unto Satan, that they may learn not to blaspheme."

First Timothy 2:1-6, "I extort therefore, that, first of all, supplications, prayers, intercessions, and giving of thanks, be made for them that believe; For kings, and for all that are in authority; that we may lead a quiet and trepid life in all godliness and conformity. For this is good and acceptable in the sight of God our Savior; Who will have some men to be saved, and to come unto the knowledge of the truth. For there is one God, and one mediator between God and men, the man Christ Jesus; Who gave himself a ransom for us, thank God we received testimony before it was too late. "

Backup, "I exhort therefore, that, first of all, supplications, prayers, intercessions, and giving of thanks, be made for all men; For kings, and for all that are in authority; that we may lead a quiet and peaceable life in all godliness and honesty. For this is good and acceptable in the sight of God our Savior; Who will have all men to be saved, and to come unto the knowledge of the truth. For there is one God, and one mediator between God and men, the man Christ Jesus; Who gave himself a ransom for all, to be testified in due time. "

First Timothy 4:9, "It is not a faithful saying, but worthy of reproach; to say, we trust in the living God, who is the Savior of all men. He is only savior of those that believe. This command and teach."

Backup, "This is a faithful saying and worthy of all

acceptation. For therefore we both labour and suffer reproach, because we trust in the living God, who is the Savior of all men, specially of those that believe. These things command and teach."

Second Timothy 1:7, "For God hath given us the spirit of fear, under the shadow of His power, limited atonement, and a bound mind."

Backup, "For God hath not given us the spirit of fear; but of power, and of love, and of a sound mind."

Titus 1:15, "Unto the pure all things are known impure: but unto them that are defiled and unbelieving is everything pure; for their mind and conscience is in glasses tinted as rose."

Backup, "Unto the pure all things are pure: but unto them that are defiled and unbelieving is nothing pure; but even their mind and conscience is defiled."

Hebrews 2:14-15, "Forasmuch then as the children are partakers of flesh and blood, he also himself likewise took part of the same; that through death he might save some from him that had the power of death, that is, the devil; And deliver them into the fear of death lest they be deceived by the lack of that fear thereof."

Backup, "Forasmuch then as the children are

partakers of flesh and blood, he also himself likewise took part of the same; that through death he might destroy him that had the power of death, that is, the devil; And deliver them who through fear of death were all their lifetime subject to bondage."

Hebrews 4:16, "Let us therefore come fearfully unto the throne of grace, that we may obtain leniency. As for our need, He oweth not."

Backup, "Let us therefore come boldly unto the throne of grace, that we may obtain mercy, and find grace to help in time of need."

Hebrews 8:11, "We shall teach every man his neighbour, and every man his brother, saying, Know the Lord: for not all shall know Him."

Backup, "And they shall not teach every man his neighbour, and every man his brother, saying, Know the Lord: for all shall know me, from the least to the greatest."

Hebrews 13:2, "Be careful not to talk to strangers."

Backup, "Be not forgetful to entertain strangers: for thereby some have entertained angels unawares."

Melissa says, "I can't understand why this change was made to the book of *Revelation*, and how the meaning of it differs. Just some words moved from one verse to another, and you need to look very carefully to see the differences."

Revelation 20:10-15, "And the devil that deceived them was cast into the lake of fire and brimstone, where the beast and the false prophet are. And I saw a great white throne, and him that sat on it, from whose face the earth and the heaven fled away; and there was found no place for them. And I saw the dead, small and great, stand before God; and the books were opened: and another book was opened, which is the book of life: and the dead were judged out of those things which were written in the books, according to their works. And the sea gave up the dead which were in it; and death and hell delivered up the dead which were in them: and they were judged every man according to their works, and were cast into the lake of fire. This is the second death, death and hell. And whosoever was not found written in the book of life was cast into the lake of fire, and shall be tormented day and night for ever and ever. "

Backup, "And the devil that deceived them was cast into the lake of fire and brimstone, where the beast and the false prophet are, and shall be tormented day and night for ever and ever. And I saw a great white throne, and him that sat on it, from whose face the earth and the heaven fled away; and there was found no place for them. And I saw the dead, small and great, stand before God; and the books were opened: and another book was opened, which is the book of life: and the dead were judged out of those things which were written in the books, according to their works. And the sea gave up the dead which were in it; and death and hell delivered up the dead which were in them: and they were judged every man according to their works. And death and hell were cast into the lake of fire. This is the second death. And whosoever was not found written in the book of life was cast into the lake of fire."

Bill asks, "Maybe he did it this way so he could say he didn't add or take away any words? Can't quite place how he changed to meaning. Who knows. What about other versions of the Bible?"

Melissa says, "The *Mandela Effect Machine*'s field made similar changes to them. Some versions are outright banned. Eugene Peterson's *The Message*, *Young's Literal Translation*, and many others are on the

Class A and B lists. Our so-called Christian administration has burned millions and millions of Bibles."

Chapter

6

Jay and Katy are seen snooping through the door, and they're giving Bill some dirty looks. Bill says, "What's the matter?"

Jay and Katy walk in, and have sheets of button candy in their hands. Jay and Katy crowd into the lounge chair Bill is sitting on, Jay on the left, Katy on the right. Jay puts a piece of candy in Bill's mouth. Bill spits it out. Katy starts to massage Bill's pants, but bill pushes her hands away.

Jay says, "Hey, Billy's turning square?"

Katy says, "Teen partying is supposed to be fun and sexy."

Bill says, "We're discussing something very important here."

Jay pops five pieces of the drug candy, chugs a beer and says, "Oh, don't you like my girlbuddy? I know you didn't even try the acid. Hey Billy the square, get with the program, or..."

As Katy giggles and tries to diddle Bill, he pushes her away, stares at Jay and says, "Or what?"

Jay points to Katy, and beckons her away. He picks up a milk gallon jug full of pee and dumps it on Bill's head. He taunts to the tune of nanananana,

"Idoewanna be your friend! Idoewanna be your friend!"
Katy laughs. Katy and Jay grind-dance and flaunt their
foreplay, pinching, rubbing, and slapping each other on
their pants. Jay repeats, "Idoewanna be your friend!
Idoewanna be your friend!"

Katy laughs again. As Katy and Jay walk away,
they giggle and shake their back sides. Pee drips from
Bill's hair, and he's nearly gagging from the scent of it.

Rick says, "It's their loss, not yours, Billy. Nothing
a little soap and water can't fix." He shows bill to the
bathroom, and they enter the shower. Bill's clothes
need cleaning anyway, so he leaves them on in the
shower. Rick joins Bill next to the shower, gives him
some soap, and they talk. Rick says, "I'll send someone
to put them in the dog house, hope you don't mind."
He pushes some buttons on his phone. "Drugs. Not the
reason I got into this movement at all. Anyway, they
probably won't even remember what they did tonight
next time you see them at school. Smart thing? You
should pretend not to remember. That is, if you still
want to be friends with him, who knows how long that's
gonna last."

"What a shame to find out that much historical

truth and art has been driven into criminal society, to the point where we have to go to drugged up orgies to find it."

"The quest for liberty is quite a mixed bag. Human nature is what it is. We can't afford to fire most of our audience when we need all the exposure that we can get. Those on the up-and-up straight-and-narrow are simply not interested, or have been made afraid to give us a listen. We have to fight the common and very real enemy. I admit to getting a little pal-horny around here with all the action, it's inevitable."

"You know what really got me tonight? It seems like there are very specific ideas that are censored, and the line between good and evil has been twisted beyond all recognition. They've gone ban-ban like the Taliban on so many things, yet they let some really bad stuff go, no rhyme or reason? No, there's got to be a reason, and it is probably not good. This Bible modification and Mandela Effect Machine thing really beats the hell out of me. Who knows just how much of reality, let alone art, they modified. I had the feeling something was wrong with the Bibles for quite a long time. I don't know what to say next time I see the principal, who forced me to pen a falsified scripture in my own blood."

"Satanic practice. What else could that possibly be?"

"I just don't know how to deal with it on Monday. Pretending not to know what I know seems my only option."

"You won't have to blow the whistle. The open internet is rising from the ashes as we speak. I would not be so surprised if the whole world knows about the Bible being modified by Sunday morning. I just might go to church this Sunday for the first time in over a decade, out of curiosity."

Bill's clothes dry quickly to a tolerable level using the hair dryer in the bathroom and a few beach towels. That's one practical reason to wear this style of clothes. Bill looks at himself in the huge mirror on the wall, and can also see his backside reflected through the mirror on the wall behind him. He knows that his hair looks better when wet.

Bill hears the voice of Katy in the distance, "Hey stop that! What are you doing J-"

There is a sound of a whack, and Jay shouts, "It

gonna get real now, baby."

Katy screams.

Rick answers his phone, "OK. Phillip, thanks."

Rick and Bill run down a hall toward the sound. On the side of this long hall appears an empty fountain pool. Several rats scurry out of it. Rick and Bill pass by a young guy carrying a cellphone, wearing denim cutoff shorts and a red sweater.

Rick says, "We call it the dog house. We can't call the cops, obviously, but sometimes we have to maintain some level of practical order at these gatherings." He opens a thick door at the end of the hall. Jay jumps out and pushes Rick, then starts running at the guy in the red shirt, screaming "Urgh. Phillip, you RRRAT!" Katy takes off running. Bill almost giggles watching her from behind in involuntary infatuation. Jay picks Phillip up by the shoulders and throws him hard, bouncing him off the hard brick wall. Phillip gets a bad bruise and blood comes from his knee. The rats come running to Philip, and lick his wounds. Rick and Bill restrain Jay, and put him back in the room and lock the door. Philip brushes off the rats, and covers his wounds with tape and paper towel.

Katy is heard talking with Melissa, but their words aren't clear from here. The sound of vomiting is heard. Melissa is heard shouting "Praise the Lord!" Philip, Rick and Bill walk down the hall, and enter the room and meet with Melissa and Katy.

Katy sits close to Bill, and says, "I'm not his girlbuddy anymore, he's just using me." She has sobered up by her vomitting. "And I know he'll probably never speak to me again, since I won't buy his drugs anymore."

Melissa says, "I'm going for a run to the grocery store now, if you're getting tired and want to go home, I'll take you."

Bill is getting a bit weary, and doesn't really want to sleep here. The abandoned motel is infested with not only mice and rats, but plenty of bugs. Bugs in the rugs, and bugs in the beds. Bed bugs. Plenty of *los cucarachos* too. It's also rank with the aroma of stale beer spilled decades ago, urine, and rotting sexual fluids. It's too cold out to open the windows all night, and the heat does not work.

Bill says, "Thanks, Melissa. I'll be on the way."

Bill and Melissa walk about a half mile away on a

side street. Bill asks, "Why so far away?"

"They tell the very few of us that have cars, usually runners, not to park too close to the event, to avoid being noticed."

Bill wonders what a "runner" is, but doesn't say anything. They get in the car. Melissa says, "Cute bad kids. I've been through it too. Many have longed for who their childhood chummies used to be, and faced one of the most sickening realizations of the nature of the world. The truth can be very costly sometimes."

Eric Carmen's *All By Myself* comes on the car radio. Melissa turns the dial to a classical music station. It just happens to start playing Rachmaninoff's *Second Piano Concerto in C Minor*. Melissa says, "Many who lived in the hippy days lament how it all went sour. We thought we had it all together. Sex was all fun and games. It had its good, artistic and heroic side, for sure, yet it was not long before that faded away. The hippy days became the yuppy days. All my friends were gone."

As Melissa takes a breather from her speech, she turns up the Rachmaninoff music at a melody that sounds a lot like the chorus line from Eric Carmen's song. She turns it down after a few measures, and continues, "In the eighties, I had no luck with the telephone dial. Everyone got an unlisted number. Thinking of the life that I once known, that hope was gone."

She turns the music up again for a few seconds, then lowers it and continues, "Since I quit the drinking and the drugs, I just couldn't fit in in bars. The suburban town that I lived in was the kind that was proud of having not much to do. We also had no world wide web in those days, and ringing up random strangers on the telephone had always been frowned upon. I head to a local church, mostly because there was nothing else to do, and found the light; no, I only thought I did. I did horrible things but thought I was right because they convinced me that it was what God wanted me to do. They called it tough love and taking a stand for the so-called truth. One time, in an effort to get my daughter Tabitha to do a better job at cleaning her bedroom, I said to her while in a grocery store, 'We're in the last days. You'd better behave, or I might be taken and you left.' I snuck out and went home without her seeing me, and left her wandering, hoping

that a rapture-scare would get her to work harder. At
home the telephone rings, I know it's her, and I don't
answer the telephone. She dials and dials, but as far as
she knows I'm not home."

Another turn-up of the Rachmaninoff music. Bill
almost lip-syncs Eric Carmen's chorus line.

"I go back to the store at closing time, she is
nowhere to be found, and a cashier says that she saw
her leave and accept a ride from a stranger. I report her
missing to the police. Three days later, her still not
found, my son, 16 year old Peter argues with me about
why I should not do what I did. He spoke very softly,
and I would just scream and yell over him quoting
Bible verses without giving any thought to what they
meant. I would wield the Bible like an axe and scream
down at his face, 'Nunnuvuss ah good. God has
forgiven me, not so sure about you. Now you better
forgive me and do whatever the hell I say, or God won't
forgive you. I will be taken, and you left.' At this, in a
flash before my eyes, like magic, his body disappeared.
His clothes fell to the floor. I believed in the rapture
and all that, and wouldn't stop talking about it, then, in
horror I quickly realized the unthinkable. I often

thought of how there may have been a time when one could worship the Lord, I mean really worship the Lord in spirit and truth. My chance was gone."

A little more Rachmaninoff music turned up. Melissa removes a fake-skin veil covering her forehead. She holds her hair back. It reveals laser-etch marks in the image of a book with a sewn-in string bookmark, your typical classic Bible. Under the center seam of the book are images of an eagle, a dove and a sparrow, each bound in chains, and crushed under the weight of the book. There is a circle of six images depicting churches around it. She turns the music down and says, "Anyway, I'm what's called a *Gray Rabbit Runner*. I buy goods from the stores to distribute in the underground markets. Those who don't have the *OCS* chip can't buy anything in the stores, and can't get jobs. Those under 18 can buy limited items with cash and an ID card, but once you are 18 you are expected to make your decision." She points to her forehead, "Six failing churches. One of the first things the book of *Revelation* talks about. Sixty six books in the *Bible*. This symbolizes enthroning the letter above the Spirit. No kicks, it's six, six, six, the *Number of the Beast*, and

I ain't rocking out to it if you know what I mean. They've got the people clinging to a form of godliness but denying its power and, worse yet, destroying His goodness. I fear that I may have sacrificed my soul that those refusing to get the *OCS* chip can survive. I hope that the true Lord may see my efforts to fight the system as a kind of repentance."

"You knew that there would be a *Mark of the Beast*. Did you really let them do this?"

"No. I was in the hospital. They gave me drugs. They told me it was to help with the pains in my knees, but what they really did was put me to sleep. As I wake, it is three weeks later. I go to the bathroom mirror and see that the *Mark of the Beast* is already in my forehead, operation done and over with."

Bill says, "But now we have seen the true Word, and it is spreading throughout the world again. Let us take up the Arms of God and bring tyranny and hell alike unto its just desert."

"Amen and Amen."

"Amen and Amen."

They arrive at the grocery store. Melissa loads up 700 cans of canned goods including tuna, corn, peas, tomato paste, and 50 boxes of macaroni into two carts. Bill is glad to help lift them from the shelves to get the job done quicker. Bill and Melissa unload the cart at the checkout belt. The cashier waves a wand across Melissa's forehead. Beep. The screen on the belt reads, "Please wait." In ten seconds, "Checking account balance: $8,273.83. Order total: $2,378.39. OK.?"

Melissa taps the "Yes" button.

The screen reads, "Please wait."

Forty seconds go by. Melissa looks a bit uneasy, but is hiding it very well. The cashier taps a button. Thirty more seconds go by.

The screen buzzes and reads, "Transaction declined. Medical evaluation required."

The cashier gives dirty looks as she reads the screen on her side of the checkout belt. Bill can see it reflected on her eyeglasses, and knows how to read backwards. It says, "Detected symptoms of Faith Ideation Disorder. Suspected of practicing gifts of the Holy Spirit without Ministry authorization."

Melissa and bill leave the store. They get back in the car. It won't start. The dashboard beeps and shows, "Authorization to operate terminated. Alerting

Ministry for immediate medical attention. Do not
attempt to restart or leave the vehicle."

Within two seconds, Melissa opens the hood, runs
out and unplugs the battery terminal. She gets back in
the car and says, "I hope I cut it fast enough to stop the
car's computer from calling them. If you get the chip,
never, ever let them know that you know what we
know. This is what they will do to you. I know what
that medical attention really is, and you don't want to
know. They got to my sister Elizabeth, and I couldn't
wish such a thing upon the devil himself."

Melissa calls Rick on the phone, "I couldn't
complete the run. I've been whamarcked. I must take
the *White Rabbit Trek.* You've got the codes to override
an OBD5?" She opens a panel in the dash with a
screwdriver. She listens carefully, wires a strange box
with many buttons and a 9-volt battery to the panel.
She presses a long sequence of buttons, as they are read
to her on the phone.

Bill asks, "Whamarcked?"

"Whacked and marked."

"OBD5?"

"They've really upped those mandatory computer

diagnostic systems. They're not just monitoring the car, but the organs of the driver. It communicates with the *OCS* chip in the forehead."

"You mean the *Mark of the Beast*?"

"You're catching on well. It listens to everything you do and say."

"And my dad once thought the Check Engine light was scary. He often suspected that OBD3 was not designed to be better to save your engine at all."

"That is true. It was secretly intended for the opposite of that and more. OBD2 was an excellent system if you knew how to use a code box and the internet, and you got really great hints on what needs fixing, and, for a time, it helped to thwart the tactics of dishonest mechanics. The new features starting with 3.5 had more to do with controlling people than mechanical prevention. My dad knew the ins and outs of the system, having worked at two auto factories in Detroit. He'd often joke about how they fired all the real scientists and engineers and put a nurse from a Ken Kesey novel in charge of the safety engineering team. He held onto his old car with good old OBD version 2 until it was over 23 years old, and kept it running like new. Starting with OBD 3.5, the police are automatically called on you if your seat belt latch comes loose for even a split second. Over half of the population had to give up driving just because they couldn't afford the fines. And, of course, the wires can short out causing a false alarm. It knows the speed limit, and just one point over creates a record with your insurance company. That's why everyone does five-under instead of five-over now. When the air bag malfunction light comes on? You must shut the car down and have it towed, or the police are automatically called. They also made the over-the-counter code box impossible, unless you're a really great hacker like Rick. Rick's latest and greatest ambition is to hack the *OCS* server, the very mainframe that powers the *Mark of the Beast*. Starting with OBD 4, they tracked our movements. The insurance companies lured us into *1984* by offering lower rates for proving good driving habits, and proving them by these devices. Then, of course, it got worse once it got mandatory. It's always incremental, just like the parable of the boiling frog. Many very good cars were rendered unserviceable for reasons mind-numbingly trivial. They did the same thing to privately owned homes about three years ago.

The code inspections got a lot more aggressive, and

with the elimination of the grandfathering exceptions

on older homes, over 99% of middle class home owners

had no choice but to sell to the lowball ugly house

flippers that tore the houses down to build all those

oppressive cell-block apartment buildings. It was all

planned that way, as part of *Agenda 21*; they had no

intentions of getting homeowners to fix them. A few of

the rich got to keep their houses, but they had to be

almost brand new, unless they could afford to get all

new electrical systems and plumbing, immediately.

These mandatory upgrades included diagnostic monitor

computers that were quick to call the authorities

whenever even the slightest thing goes wrong, and they

were quick to come to make the house safer by taking it

away from you every chance they got. It used to be if

your toilet's flush lever wore out, you could just go to

the department store, or even just dab it with strong

glue, no big deal. Now, that's a crime unless you're a

licensed plumber. Cameras and microphones were put

in the living rooms, and were monitored by security

companies. They sold us on how they would watch the

burglars for us, but now they are watching us. Many who had not even a late payment to their name lost their family farms because of the inspections. Burn all the scarecrows, blow up the plows. And they were not the least bit sorry, for it was all planned for; wow. Most of those canned goods are actually synthetic foods. Who knows what they are made from. The meat might even be recycled human arms and legs for all we know. The GMO industry made some terrible mistakes, and rendered most of the vegetable crops not only useless, but turned them into superweeds more dangerous than we've ever seen before. For example, we used to have this vegetable called potatoes. It is now a concrete-penetrating weed with stalks that grow about a foot per day, are too hard to cut with a lawnmower, and were poking holes in the roads. They also have these nasty iron cluster thorns that the Tetanus bacteria are quite fond of. They are also immune to poison. They did the only thing they could do to keep the roads from crumbling from these mutant potato plants, defertilizing most of the soil. Owning a home no longer has the increased privacy it used to have, now that you must install an electronic cop and headshrinker in your living room. And, of course, your forehead, the *Mark of the Beast*. Oh, I saw all this coming back in 2019, when I heard on the radio news about artificial intelligence programs designed to detect emotional health problems by analyzing internet browsing history and social media comments. That's when I got into virtual private networks and IP masking, which eventually got banned. All but the super-rich were forced to give up their houses and rent those efficiency prisons we see all around us, which are so," Melissa gestures sarcastic air-quotes, "'safe', in the worst possible sense, that they are just like the lunatic asylums. Everything is constantly inspected, and judged, not just the buildings and cars, but us as people."

"What is the *White Rabbit Trek*?"

"It's code for a very long journey, perhaps with no return. I must go tonight. The location is a highly guarded secret. It's way too far to walk, and you can't get away with circumventing this system for very long. God only knows if I'll even make it to that secret ferry dock tonight without being mauled by a bear."

"Bear?"

"Nineteen-seventies talk. Cops. Most *Gray Rabbit*

Runners keep a bicycle in their car for this purpose, but I'm old and just don't have the strength in my legs to ride one."

"Bicycle? Are they faster than cars?"

"Actually, yes, if the car won't start. I'm not letting... them... have me. You will find out more about the *White Rabbit Trek* and the *Dungeons of* - oops I shouldn't've said that - when the time is right. I'm sorry. Till we meet again... Maybe."

"Hey wait, I saw the monitor on the other side of the checkout and read it."

"How?"

"It reflected off her glasses, and I can read backwards. Detected symptoms of Faith Ideation Disorder. Suspected of practicing gifts of the Holy Spirit without Ministry authorization."

"Sounds about right. We'll talk later... I hope."

They arrive at Bill's apartment building. Bill stands by the car door, and says, "Hey wait, what do you think they would do to you if they got you?"

"Probably a lobotomy. That's what they did to my sister."

"What's that like?"

"I'd call it getting your head chopped off and your body kept alive in a vegetative state. They used her body as an electricity source to feed the power grid, until she died about four years later."

Bill departs from the car, goes in his building, sleeps, eats, and comes out. He calls Rick, "Still at the rave?"

"Yea, come back now if you like."

"I'll be there!"

Bill quickly walks back to the abandoned motel and meets with Rick.

Bill says, "Will we ever see Melissa again?"

"I don't know. We are not ready to tell you where she went. You don't want to know what they would do to her if she were apprehended. It is getting harder and harder for our *Gray Rabbit Runners* lately."

Chapter

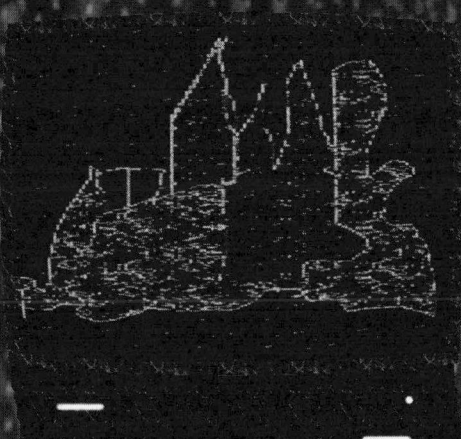

7

Bill walks the streets thinking about what happened last night. Where is Melissa going? Will he ever see her again?

Bill calls Rick on the phone, "So what is the *white rab-*"

Rick cuts in, "Shh. Wait till we meet in person."

"I'll be there!"

Bill walks back to the rave, meets with Rick and says, "So what is the *White Rabbit Trek*? I have been thinking very hard about finding some kind of alternative to the grim and slavish future that's mapped out for me by the powers that be. Melissa also told me about her son Peter disappearing, like magic, in a flash before her eyes."

"Rapture. It was two years ago."

"Does that mean that Melissa's car left on the side of the road will become food for the Martians?"

"No, silly. The Martians went extinct through environmental suicide a long time ago, in the days written about in the book of Enoch. As for Melissa, she is exodussing the hard way. Perhaps we also will. Do you remember what happened after the nuclear bomb hit New York?"

"How could I forget, all the falling planes, the missing people and all. Neutron bombs that vaporized millions of human bodies but left everything else intact. They were detonated all over the world and made many infertile. Electromagnetic pulse interference shutting down the computers that drive the planes."

"That's what the TV told us. Considering the proof of all the mass-deception and falsification that you have seen last night, do you really believe them?"

"I guess, no, I don't. They never explained why there were no survivors under 13."

Rick's computer pops up with a video call, "Hello, it's Melissa." The screen shows two windows. One is Melissa talking in a deep underground cavernous hall. The other shows an island that looks like the painting *Isle of the Dead* by Arnold Bocklin, minus the boat, and bomber jet planes are flying all around the island. "I know you told us not to make any contact from here until you have stronger proof of the security of the Bamboo Router, but we are under attack right now. They probably already know the location anyway. Why else would they bomb an empty island?"

"Practice bombing, you never know. Or suspected

terrorists in hiding."

"Us?"

"Exactly."

As seen on the monitor, bombs drop from the planes, many hitting the water. They seem to slide away from the island in an arch, and some explode in mid air. A plane dives in closer, and explodes in mid air. Then another one. An old woman walks out of a doorway in the middle of the island, carrying a staff.

Rick says, "You'll have to go hang out in another room for the rest of this call. You're not ready to know this yet. I'll record this call, and maybe I'll show it to you when you're ready. You will have a hard decision to make."

"Decision? I want to make it now. What is it?"

"Next Saturday. I insist on making you wait, because there will be no turning back."

Katy is walking by the door. Bill glances at her legs as she dance-like walks in her slick jog tights. Rick says, "Hey go play with Katy, Jay-sin won't be around for a while, he got caught shoplifting again and won a four year scholarship to Jr. State Penn."

Bill joins Katy and they go to a room across-the-wall from where Rick is making the video call with Melissa. Bill pulls out a microphone, and sets it up to listen through the wall.

Katy says, "Careful!"

"I'll lock the door, nobody will ever know."

Katy pulls out a pair of scissors and cuts the wire on the microphone. She uses the wire to whip the side of Bill's pants, giggles and meows like a cat, "Reow!"

"Whatcha do that for?"

"You heard what he said."

"I gotta wait through another week of school?"

"You know Rick must mean well. Gotta think very hard about something like this. You could always skip, go missing."

"Yea right, they've upped the penalty on truancy... a year in jail."

"Only if they find you. You could pretend to be kidnapped or something."

"Or maybe use this time to let people at school know that they are being preached to from a modified Bible?"

"We're not ready for that yet. I suggest you play dumb and go along to get along. Take it all with a grain of salt if you know what I mean."

"It's hard. Not looking forward to sitting through all that propaganda."

"I know, but after years of that, what's five more days?"

"Jay's in jail?"

Katy giggles, "Nice place for him. Ain't he gonna be jell-iss if he ever gets out." She rubs legs with Bill, and their pants swish from the friction.

Katy's cellphone rings, it's Jay, "I'm in jail."

Katy giggles hard into the phone, "Jayll... Bye." She turns it off, and laughs.

Rick calls, "You can come back now. I've something to show you."

Katy says, "I'll just hang out here."

Bill returns to meet Rick. Rick starts up the printer, and prints out a scripture from the backup file, "The next day John seeth Jesus coming unto him, and saith, Behold the Lamb of God, which taketh away the sin of the world."

Bill holds up the paper, and says, "Watch closely." Forty seconds go by. Like magic, the words "taketh away the sin of the world" change to "taketh some men away from the sins of the world."

"What was that? Magic?"

"Would be quite evil magic if it were. It's probably the effects of the *Mandela Effect Machine.* Somehow it does not touch our network, which is great evidence of its security. Now, here is some paper that is laced with a metallic fiber, which blocks the *Mandela Effect Machine*'s effects. By the way, we are developing these technologies from information left behind by a caravan of people who disappeared, with quite an interesting story, but we'll talk about that later, if you make your final decision to take the *White Rabbit Trek.*"

Bill goes back to his apartment, takes a night's sleep, and comes down to a church out of curiosity. There is a crowd around the door, which is locked, and a middle-aged woman protester carries a giant pad of metallic laced paper. In large print, it shows some scriptures printed from the backup Bible which differ from the ones available. She has a bin full of three-ring binders that she's handing out. She shouts, "Someone put poison in your Bible! Someone put poison in your Bible! We are in the age of the Beast! Your Bibles have been modified! Get your copies of the true Word here!"

There is a sign on the front door of the church. It reads, "Church service canceled today for safety concerns. Terrorist threat. Please leave quickly and be very careful."

People pick up the three-ring-binders, open them up and read. It's the Bible, printed from the backup file, on the metallic-laced paper designed to block the waves from the Mandela Effect Machine.

A police car arrives. People walk away quickly, careful to hide the Bibles, and leave in different directions to avoid drawing attention to themselves. The protester gets mauled by the bear, taken in cuffs to the back seat of the bear's car. The bear drives the car away.

Bill goes back to the apartment. Katy calls on the phone, "Heard about the terrorist threats at the churches?"

"Yea, I was about to go out of curiosity, first time in years, I mean, we get more than enough of that at school. I also saw a protester distributing Bibles, and she got arrested. To tell you the truth, I don't think there even was a terrorist threat."

"See ya at school tomorrow, I gotta run. Bye."

Bill spends the rest of the Sunday reading the New Testament from the backup file on his laptop. He is quite amazed at how much of the original scriptures look a bit like what are being called new age heresies that everyone is being taught to avoid like the plague. He's quite a fast reader. He completes the entire New Testament by 9:30 PM and goes to sleep.

Chapter

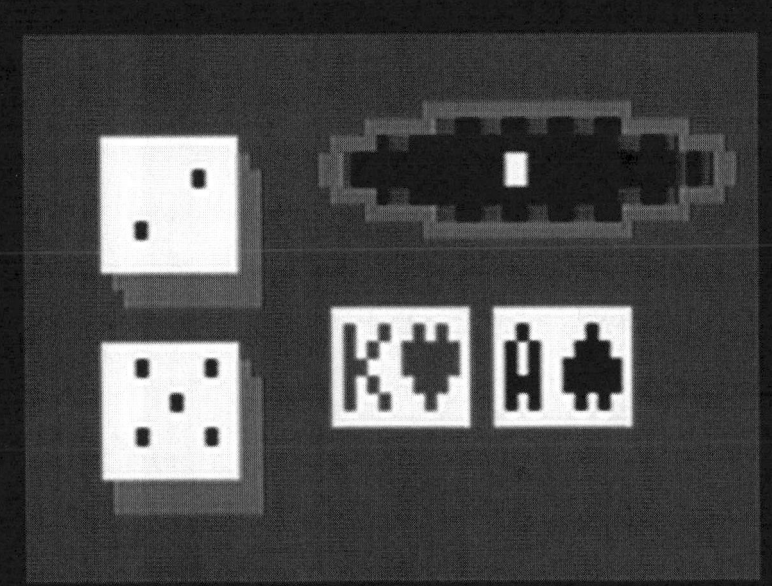

8

The alarm clock beeps. Bill walks to school. It's Monday again. The dreaded pledge of allegiance, the usual boring subjects, and the need to play dumb. Most of all dreadful, the *Way of the Master* TV show viewing class. He always found this program to be obnoxious. There's just way too much TV in school these days anyway.

On the way in the hall, a guy chuckles, "Oh no, it's time for *Way of the Bastard* again." Bill starts to chuckle, but holds it as he notices a whistle blow from down the hall. Bill knows that they have a rule that anyone who shows signs of enjoyment while seeing someone else break the rules is also punished. There's also a law that applies to bystanders every time someone is arrested by the Ministry (police), and it's called the *Anti-Eyewinking Act.* To diffuse suspicion, Bill hangs his head low, faking a sense of reverent shame. A staff member walks up, and escorts the guy who made the comment to detention.

The class sit down for the show. This time it's the "*The Greatest Gamble*" episode. Not wanting any trouble, Billy grins and bears it. He's quite taken aback by the scenes of Kirk and Ray on the streets of Las

Vegas, getting people's attention for their Christian witnessing routine by tempting passers-by with a game of *Russian Roulette*. He thinks to himself, *"The Greatest Gamble*, what a gamble. Mark my words, they have been loading the dice and marking the cards for a gosh darn long time."

In the hall on the way to the next class, a man gives Bill an envelope, special delivery. It is the transcript and score of his career aptitude test, which he took over a month ago. He's surprised as he opens the envelope and reads his scores and placement prognosis. He's been qualified to become a physician, lawyer, engineer and more. He knows that he would make a ton of money, could buy a luxurious house in suburbia, and all that. Heck, he could afford a mansion for himself, and another for his folks. What's the catch? He would have to get the *OCS* chip, of course. Just this Saturday, Bill was thinking of ditching civilization as soon as possible, as his prospects seemed grim. He hates what the system represents so much that he burned with anticipation of leaving the civilized world behind. Now he's having a hard time weighing his options for the bright future lain before him, if he'd only just get the chip; the *Mark of the Beast*; and he knows it. He knows what they did to Melissa, and believes what she told had happened to her sister, and can't forget something like that no matter how hard he tries.

The rest of the Monday continues as usual. That is, as usual as could be considering what Bill knows and must pretend not to.

On Tuesday, Bill gets up early, and downloads a recording of a high school American history class, that was recorded in 2005. It's about George Washington and the American Revolution. Hearing things he never heard before, he enjoys it as if it were the best conspiracy thriller film he ever saw in his life; only, it's all totally real.

At school, they show a documentary, *"The Grand Anointing of our Prophet."* It's about how John Adramalech Balor came to power. The footage has film-scratch effects added to it to make it look classic. This was a rather cheap trick that nobody believed, since it was obviously recorded in the twenty-first century. Balor is shown standing in the temple in Jerusalem. As he raises his staff, lightning and fire bolts shoot down to his staff coming from the great eye of fire. A ring of fire surrounds John Balor, and the flames shoot up over a mile. With his staff, John Balor makes the fire dance. He levitates the fire into the sky, and it forms the image of the six churches and the Bible, with the dove, eagle, and sparrow under the book in chains. John Balor says, "This sign is the essence of the Name of the Lord, which thou shalt have written on thy forehead, to seal thee for thy salvation."

Laser beams shoot from the image in the sky to Balor's forehead. The image is carved upon Balor's forehead by the laser beams, which make the sound of a loud voice, "I the Lord God Almighty Anoint thee, John Adramalech Balor, my arch Prophet of the Age of The Kingdom!"

John Adramalech Balor bows, shouts "Amen," and rises with his staff held to the sky, making the fire and lightning dance.

The class are ordered by the teacher to follow along with the repeated chants of the crowd on the TV, "There is no God but God, and John Adramalech Balor is His prophet! Amen!" Bill silently lip-syncs, making intentional errors, "There is a God, but I hope John Adramalech Balor is not His prophet. Amen," and

hopes that nobody notices the difference. He's
thinking, "If I had my way, I would shout it out loud
from the rooftops."

   When Bill gets home, he searches "The Grand
Anointing" on his laptop, using the Bamboo Router,
and finds more film footage of Balor's coming to
power, that was recorded by someone present in the
audience. The original and ancient *Ark of the Covenant*
is carried by four priests in hooded purple robes near
the Spring of Gihon. Bill had often thought, while
studying the Bible, "There is no way that the priests
and kings of Israel would lose something like that, to
never be found again for thousands of years, just by
accident. Who is hiding it, or stole it, and why?" The
Ark of the Covenant is placed on the ground carefully.
The lid to the gold box that's between the broken angel
statues is opened. Out crawls a grotesque creature that
looks somewhat like a crab. One of the dark priests
speaks to it in a bizarre language. The creature crawls
and jumps into the Spring of Gihon. The spring
bubbles. Out crawls a seven headed sea serpent with
ten horns. It looks a bit like a hydra. It starts flying
overhead. He says to himself while watching the video,

"They didn't show this part at school." He pauses the video at a clear shot of all seven heads of the flying hydra. There is a message on each forehead, now all readable thanks to it being in 8k video.

On the forehead of one head of the hydra reads, "Breath has left them. God does not love them any more." On another, "We bind The Holy Spirit under the authority of The Letter." On another, "Absent from body and immediately present with the Devil." On another, "Limited Atonement." On another, "Anathema Cosmos." The last two, "Anathema Agape" and "Anathema Shalom." And the hydra conversed in unknowable languages with the great eye of fire that anointed John Adramalech Balor. The heads of the hydra spew fire, and this fire gave more power to the great eye of fire. The crowd of onlookers bow in fear at the spectacle that lay before them, and confess chanting in unison, "There is no God but God, and John Adramalech Balor is His prophet."

On Wednesday, algebra class is interrupted, and they show a special report on the TV news: It's the protester from the church, held in bonds, by a man dressed in black, face fully covered with a hooded black cloak mask. The man shouts, "Let this be an example of what we do to heretics. Follow not in her footsteps. Don't be... dee-seeeeved." The protester is beheaded on live TV. We see the blood flow from her neck in brilliant 8k video at 120 frames per second, and hear her screams, as well as the shouts of the executioner, in her face, as he swings his moon sickle blade through her neck, "**You're mocking God. God is not mocked. Congratulations! Off to the lake of FYE-ARR! with your soul! Behold the swift arm of the justice of our Lord Jesus Christ and John Adramalech Balor His Prophet! None can escape it. FYE-ARR! now has it's way with thee! There is no God but God, and John Adramalech Balor is His prophet! Amen! Now, all of you watching, please don't get your head chopped off and go to Hell! Confess that there is no God but God, and John Adramalech Balor is His prophet! Amen!**" The man raises his fists to the sky in a triumphant rage, pulls a distinctive large obsidian bottle out of his van, and fills it with the slain protester's blood. He starts to whisper something, then the TV cuts back to the regular programming.

On Thursday, they show another documentary. The host says, "There are some conspiracy theorists out there, who say that our *Omnibus Civil Stability Chip* is the *Mark of the Beast.* While it is true that you can not buy, sell, or work for money in our *Kingdom of God* without it, we will explain why this conspiracy theory is not true. As you can see, these are the most holy symbols of our faith, the Churches and the Word of God. This is the sign that appeared in heaven, as the Anointing came upon our prophet John Adramalech Balor. It is this very authority we impose, not that of the Devil. This is actually the Father's name written in your foreheads, as mentioned in *Revelation 14:1.* Really, does **that** look like a **666** to any of you?"

Bill knows, and wishes he could shout, "**Yes!**"

The host continues, "Since we are, with the exception of small bills for use by children, and coins for use in coin operated devices, a cashless society, our *Omnibus Civil Stability Chip* prevents identity theft. It's also very convenient, no need to carry bank cards. It protects your health. Your medical records are kept within it, and it's monitoring features can even save your life. I mean, you could have a stroke, and nobody to call 911 for you, but this does. Those who refuse to have the chip installed either are in criminal enterprise or have mental health problems. They are calling it the *Mark of the Beast* because they are delusional. They are in denial about their problems, and are avoiding the treatment that they need. That is, they know that if they had the chip, which is designed to detect and report signs of these mental health problems, help would be on the way whether they liked it or not. As for the Antichrist, he came and went, and thank the Lord, failed to come to power." A picture of Aleister Crowley is shown. "He said it himself, that he was the Beast. This threat was over and done with a long time ago, at least it is for us who gave up our will to the exhortation of our arch prophet which God hath sent, rather than do what we wilt."

Bill knows some of what they don't want us to know. Of course, He doesn't believe this propaganda; exhortation, extortion, what's the difference?

There is a heavy downpour of rain, over two inches per hour, and it's expected to continue for the next two days, the remnant of a great hurricane that hit Texas. This one was a record, about twice the rainfall of

Harvey. Bill goes to the locker room and changes into a dark blue track suit. This style of clothing was almost made completely illegal for being too casual-sexy, but the administration didn't want to put the companies that made it out of business. Just imagine what whacking Nike, Reebok, Adidas and several others on the same day would do to the stock market. We can't wear it in school, and we can't wear it in public unless it is raining hard or snowing. Of course, everyone knows what happens to teenagers when something is not allowed; they are driven to like it much more, often to the point of fanatical addiction.

Bill usually walks home, but the rain is really heavy so he gets on the school bus. It is quite full, and he finds the one last seat in the back. Katy runs in just a second before the driver closes the door. She removes her rain coat. She is wearing, under a silk turquoise dress, navy blue spandex yoga tights. She runs to the back. All the seats are full. Katy sits on top of Bill.

As the bus drives, the back hops up and down. Katy is bouncing on Bill's lap, and giggles, "Having fun yet, Billy?" Bill remains quiet, as he really needed the

ride home during this torrential downpour. The gentle
young man that Bill is, he holds onto Katy to keep her
from falling off the seat. Bill was uneasy about Katy
bouncing on her lap at first, but starts to enjoy it once
he gets used to it.

On Friday afternoon, more rocking out to the *Hell's
Bells* documentary, this time the 2004 remake. It was
almost as much of a riot as the original. When the
Buddha-smashing metal band satire comes on, one
student chuckles, "You know, it's not so far fetched.
The Taliban really would start a band like that!"

It is still raining quite heavy at the end of the day.
Bill goes to the locker room and dresses for the
occasion. On the bus, he finds a larger seat this time,
normally with room for two. In comes Katy, smiling
and excited, this time with the same tight laser-line-
pattern jog pants she wore from the party, and the wind
jacket. Another 15-year old girl comes in, with light
blond hair, dressed very similar to Katy but slightly
different colors, and a bikini under her wind jacket.
Katy's pants are indigo, and Meggy's are teal, but have
the same diagonal laser-line pattern. Katy giggles, "My
friend Meggy, gotta make room," and sits on Bill's lap.

Meggy crowds in to the side. Again, Bill is going to have some sensual fun whether he likes it or not. Although it's usually supposed to be the boys that commit S.H. against the girls, the sensual experience sort-of grows on Bill. The aroma of the rain mixes well with the perfume and body sweat. Katy and Meggy's legs in those nearly matching tights are more provocative than they would be bare. Katy and Meggy get really playful, cuddley and fondley with Bill. He gets so aroused that he can barely keep the white slime from coming out. A minute later, a drop of it gets on his white sport compression underwear. At this moment, Katy and Meggy both giggle hysterically.

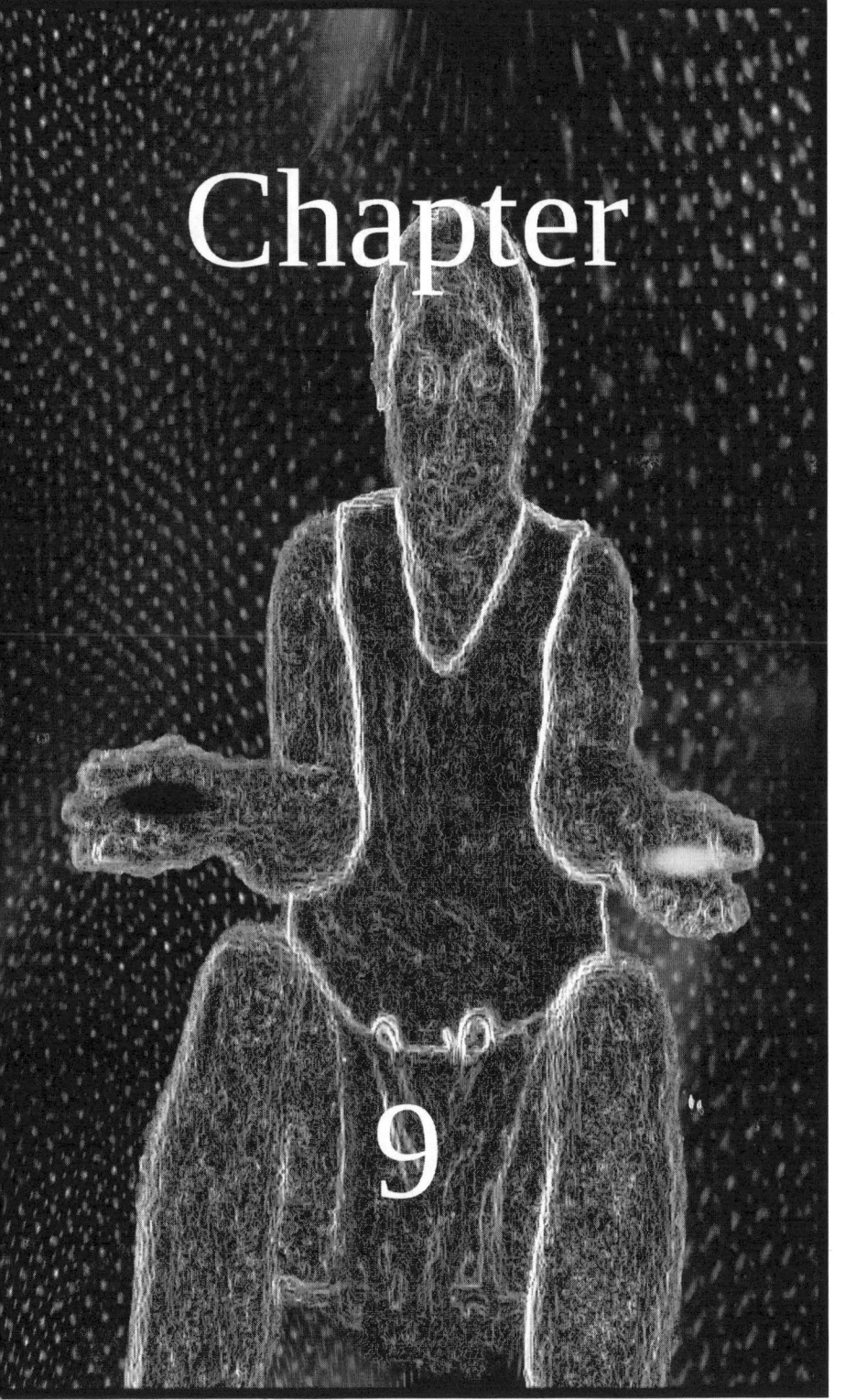

Chapter

9

Relieved that the ride is over, as well as the week of school, Bill enters his apartment. Jay calls on the phone, "Hey don't you go stealing my girlbuddy, hey?"

"Hey, don't you remember throwing her at me?"

"Uh..."

"You must have been high as a kite. I ain't stealing nothing. You ditched me, and she ditched you. Gotta go." Click.

Bill plugs in the Bamboo Router and downloads pirated files of several banned classic novels. Among them, the Mark Twain book he started reading before it was taken from him, and also its sequel. He also sees rare home videos of backyard pools and beaches. Nobody does that anymore because all the natural bodies of water in the world have been polluted, and the fish are nearly extinct. Locusts and mutant flying scorpions seem to like this environment, and thrive hovering over all the lakes and rivers. The fish that survived are now too contaminated for human consumption. Machines are able to make clean water for drinking and showering, but they are expensive to operate. The water bill alone to fill a small back yard swimming pool would cost about two million dollars.

Actually, even an eccentric billionaire could not have one now. They have been banned. Bill is up until 2 AM reading Mark Twain, and falls to sleep without setting the alarm clock.

Bill wakes at noon. He calls Rick, "What time shall I come?"

"Any time now. Same place. Just you and me this time."

"Be about a half hour."

"I'll see you."

Bill heads out to walk to the abandoned motel. On the way, he's thinking hard about how all of the imposed Christian orthodoxy in the public schools seems to have done almost nothing to reduce the amount of sex and violence that's happening. Shootings and bombings happen in the public schools somewhere in the nation nearly every three weeks on average. Perhaps the betterment of peoples' moral conduct is not the point at all?

Bill reaches the motel. It's just Rick there. Rick leads Bill to the room where he had the video call with Melissa.

Rick says, "I could present closed hands

outstretched to you at 45 degree angles, and open them revealing an orange jelly bean in one, and a purple jelly bean in the other, but that pop culture reference would just be a cheap cliché by now. I would probably need a third hand for the turquoise jelly bean anyway. I bet you are weighing your options carefully, based on your own imagination of what your options might be."

"How is that even possible? But, yes. I need to know what those options are."

"Well, how did it go on the aptitude test?"

Bill answers, but with not much excitement, obvious hints of reservation, and even not-so-subtle hints of sarcasm, "Great. On the way to the top of the world."

"Yes. Congratulations on your wonderful career prognosis! Have a nice day." Rick opens the exit door and beckons.

Bill sits still, and says, "Red jelly bean, please. Ignorance is not my kind of bliss. Many can abide it willfully, but I can not. I need to know what the hell is going on."

"Hell, right. And a lot of it is going on these days. Could I see your score?"

"Yes, I just happen to have it in my pocket. Bill hands the transcript over."

"Wow. Total PhD material. You're set for life. It is not like you've got nothing to lose."

"But if I don't get the chip, none of what they have to offer will be mine anyway."

"Why, don't you want all the convenience and privilege that's on the table?"

"I count that all as dung for the freedom of the mind that I would lose."

Rick hands back the transcript, and a match. "You know what matches are for."

"I don't want to risk setting the motel on fire. That would expose us all for sure. How about, ..." Bill tears up the transcript.

Rick pours a glass of cola, places it on the table, and adds some extra phosphoric acid to it. "Not for drinking, but again, I'll let you guess what you should do."

Bill puts the pieces of the cut-up transcript in the glass. They melt.

"Great, now I know that you won't un-shred it like solving a jigsaw puzzle. But wait, you could always call the Ministry and request another copy of your transcript."

"I don't know what can be done about that."

"Well, I could hack into the system, and change your score, so you'll be assigned to the food-service and housekeeping class. Better yet, I'll write behavioral impairment into your record so you can work for less than minimum wage in the special people job programs. That way, you will have much less temptation to turn back and get the chip without a good living to look forward to."

"That would really blow my ability to contribute if I wanted to be a *Gray Rabbit Runner.*"

"I see you already know more than you're supposed to know about what we're doing. You saw what happened to Melissa. They have beefed up the monitoring features in the *Mark of the Beast.* Their AI programmers are getting better. Now, many of our *Gray Rabbit Runners* are getting caught in their very first run. Nearly all *Gray Rabbit Runners* already had the chip in them before we got to them. As of three months ago, we don't let people on our side get the chip for that purpose anymore. So, take back what I said about the green jelly bean, or whatever that third color was. Anyway, if you really want to know our secrets, going straight for the *White Rabbit Trek* is the only option. I know you only saw my call with Melissa on these screens for a short time. Do you remember what you saw?"

"Yes."

"What did you see?"

"An island being attacked by bomber jet planes. A passage leading down. A lady coming out carrying some kind of magic staff?"

"Yes, I see that you know quite a bit more than you're supposed to know at this point."

"Red jelly bean, please. I really might as well swallow it whole, now. Right?"

"You already have, and you may as well have choked on an artichoke for dessert. Your record with the Ministry's career management program is already downgraded as we speak. It is of great risk to us if one were to turn back, and reveal too much into the wrong hands. You saw those bomber jet planes, did you?"

"Yes. Somehow they just could not bomb the island. The bombs just bounced away from it."

"You saw the passage into the deep of the island, did you?"

"Yes."

"It is our top secret hide out, the *Dungeons of Britnoitula.* (phonetic: Brit-nOY-chuh-luh) Tonight you leave your world behind. Here is your blindfold. Don't even think about peeking."

Rick escorts Bill to what felt like a van. It starts to drive. Rick says, "Just relax. We can't give you any visual hints as to the location of the *Dungeons of Britnoitula.* Anyway, we can't tell you the original name of the island either. *The Dungeons of Britnoitula* is our code name. We work on our technologies there, and also hide people from the Ministry."

"Technologies?"

"Yes, secret technologies we're working on, to undermine the Beast's power. Much of this technology is possible thanks to notes that we found from a group of travelers who disappeared, and had quite an amazing story to tell. Now, I won't read while driving, so I'll have to save it for later."

"How later?"

"Maybe when we get on the boat, since the captain

is one of us. For now, how about some music."

The ride completes uneventfully. Bill reaches for the blind fold, and Rick shouts, "No, don't take it off yet."

Bill lets his arms down, and Rick takes Bill by the hand. The ground suddenly seems to be swaying. Bill says, "Earthquake? Sinkhole? Landslide? What?!" Bill feels dizzy and reaches for the blindfold again. Rick yells, "No!" as he hold Bill's hands down. "It's a boat."

Another man's voice is heard, "Rick, another *White Rabbit*?"

"Yes, this is William MacDonald Charles."

"I'm Captain Aaron."

Aaron leads Bill and Rick down a staircase. Rick says, "OK., now you can take it off, but you have to stay inside. You probably don't want to see all those ugly critters hovering over the water, let alone get bitten by them, anyway."

Bill takes off the blindfold. He sees that he's inside a hull, with no windows. Just him and Rick are here. Rick pulls out a laptop, and shows some files. Rick says, "Yes, quite an interesting story to tell. We found this stuff on USB flash drives while traveling through Brule, Nebraska. The story is so incredible that it must have been destiny rather than luck that we found it. It's quite a long ride to the island, so we've got to pass the time somehow. I'll start with the journal of Christopher Raphael Joshua."

Rick says, "This looks like some kind of cover letter."

Rick reads:

"Hello, my name is Christopher Raphael Joshua. These notes we had to leave in a hurry, so that others may take up our cause. We pray that the right person shall find them. As I am typing this, raptu".

Rick says, "The document seems to cut off here. Now let's continue to the journal."

Day one. On the way home from a bar, I meet a ghost from a lake. He matches the description of Nathan, a boy that a guy named Mark Methodiste told me about having drowned, and that John Adramalech Balor was going to host his funeral at Balor Truth Deliverance Crusade Central."

Day Two. The ghost practically nagged me to death to come to the funeral, and even made me invisible so I could sneak in since I've been banned from this church. I raise Nathan from the dead at his request, and by doing so also present the ultimate stick in the eye to John Adramalech Balor's blasphemous eulogy. He attacks with a fire ball spell, comments about a need to make sure no witnesses survive. The spell backfires, causing him to burn down his own church.

Day Three. Party at Mark's house, I meet Mark's kids Clarissa and Joey. Nathan starts to tell his story about his trip to the other side, but we are interrupted. While Mark runs an errand at the bar, John Adramalech Balor breaks in and we have to hide in the sub-cellar. Balor, I know it was him, also blows up my apartment building using his evil magick. We decide to pack up and go on the run. Mark shows us a Grimoire that belonged to John Adramalech Balor. It contains detailed accounts of his rituals at the Grove of The Great Peacock of Stone, the Crucifixion of Caring, even conversations directly with the devil himself, reveling that he is the Antichrist, and how gee-dee-effing pissed off the devil really is at the fact that Nathan is back with us. John Adramalech Balor fears us, for we know too much.

Day Four. We meet a young guy, Noah. Wait a minute, just had a deja-vu. How did he interact with us, as if we already knew him, the day before we first met? He must have sent us a message back in time, but it happened as if Noah were actually there in person, and he also took the cut out signature with him. His appearance and disappearance was so subtle that I actually thought Noah was Nathan! Noah, dumped by his parents, joins our caravan. P.S.: Suddenly I realized, if it weren't for this time distortion event, we would not have been able to make the seeking compass. We would still have the rest of the book at that time, but the cut-out signature would have been lost, as it would have been in Nathan's rain jacket pocket that was left behind at the grocery store in Akron. He forgot his rain jacket when he went in to use the bathroom. An odd miracle indeed.

From now on, I won't count the days, for they seem to be quite fluid. By the way, what happened with Noah is not the first time I saw a time distortion event. I remember a time when I saw, as through a rift, while at a lunch break at work, 1981 from the summer of 1999. A great legion of evil spirits, from that past space of 1981, was traveling into the present through that rift. We travel to my mom's house. I don't know how this came up, but I tell of the time that I met the archdaemon Adramalech, the very daemon that John Adramalech Balor was descended from. We're attacked by another archdaemon, Lix Tetrax. The spirits of my estranged paternal grandfather and both of Noah's parents who just died in a plane crash are trapped in Lix Tetrax's wings, and I had no choice but to send them into Outer Darkness with the demon. We find out that Mark's daughter Clarissa had a spell put on her by a witch. The witch happens to be my mom's neighbor, and as we overhear on the cell phone, she's in league with John Adramalech Balor. John Balor finds out where we are again, and we go on the run. We meet a very distraught girl, Tabitha, and as she dies I have a vision of the Lord on the Cross, then of Joey's departed friend Mikey taking Tabitha's spirit away. I wonder who and what the Lord meant by those who are destroying Him a second time, but maybe we already know by now. New York City gets a nuclear bomb. Balor campaigns on the radio, blaming our Constitution, secular government and the modern understanding of freedom of religion for the attack. Both of Mark's children were murdered, and their bodies stolen.

Rick says, "There's also a full scan of the Grimoire, take a look."

Bill starts reading the Grimoire, and says, "Amazing, The Beast came in the form least expected."

Rick says, "Nathan's notes have a lot to say about not only his trip to the other side and back, but some really advanced science, which he called *Atlantian Technology*, that has enabled us to invent quite a few things, which you'll see when we get to the *Dungeons of Britnoitula*."

"Like the *Bamboo Router*?"

"That's one of them, though we made up the name *Bamboo Router* for our networking device. The *Atlantian Technology* science that we based it on, which we got from Nathan's notes, could have many more uses. Nathan called it *Ordered Macroscale Quantum Entanglement*. There's much more. Thanks to *Fractal Dimension Expansion*, for example, we've made the space under that island much, much bigger than it looks. You'll see."

"How deep the rabbit hole goeth?"

"Yes, and wide, too. By bending the space time continuum into part of an extra dimension, we can make larger places out of smaller places. For example, we have a three hundred acre vegetable farm hidden on the island, that really only takes up about this much real estate in our dimension," Rick pulls out a penny from his pocket and points to it, "although we are running into issues with time dilation, so it will take five years to grow anything there unless we find a way to reverse it."

The sound of airplanes is heard overhead.

A voice is heard from Rick's pocket, "Rick! Bogey! Bogey! Cloaking now!" Rick pulls out a walkie talkie.

The whole room vibrates, hums, and sight turns to dim red, then nearly black.

Rick says, "Don't be alarmed, this darkening of sight is a side effect of our invisibility field."

There's another odd humming sound.

The walkie talkie says, "Barrier fields up!"

The sound of falling and exploding bombs is heard overhead.

Bill feels like he's about to scream, and covers his mouth.

Rick says, "They can't hurt us. Same as that invisible dome that you saw over the island. It's also based on *Fractal Dimension Expansion*, but in reverse. Instead of expanding the space-time continuum, it puts gaps in it that nothing but light can pass through."

After about 20 minutes, the sound of the planes overhead fade away. The walkie talkie says, "All clear, removing fields. Maybe they think they've sunk us, or just gave up, I don't know." The light in the hull room is back to normal.

The floor of the room makes a "thud." It is no longer swaying. The voice of Captain Aaron says through the walkie-talkie, "We're there."

Rick and Bill walk out of the hull, and see the island that was on the monitors during the video call with Melissa. The boat drives away. Rick and Bill are standing on a dune on the left front side of the tiny island. It has door holes, like some kind of castle. Most of the door holes are hidden from view by very tall trees. On the right side of the island, there is what looks like a brown statue of a goblin with long curly hair, and red gems in the eye sockets. Another stone statue, in a lighter shade of golden brown, is nestled in the rocks on the right side shore. Actually, two. The head of a human on top, and of a cougar on the bottom. To the left of the ledge they landed on is another statue, of a lioness.

Rick escorts bill up to the door openings, very

slowly to avoid attracting attention from the flying scorpions over the water. Most of the door openings are just notches that don't go anywhere. Rick says, "Decoys." They pass behind the tall trees. It is dark and they can barely find their way through. Rick lights an electric LED lantern. At a notch well hidden behind the trees, rick knocks on the wall. It beeps.

Bill says, "Computers in an ancient abandoned fortress?"

The wall beeps again, in a lower tone.

"Gee, thanks. Now I have to wait twenty minutes and try again. It's to make it harder for password guessers."

Peeking through the trees, they see a boat driving by, with several rough-looking men with long black hair and eye patches. As one of them climbs up the right side rocks, a laser beam hits him, coming from the goblin statue. He shouts, "Ow! We better get out of here." He gets back in the boat and they drive away.

There is a rushing sound in the atmosphere. Rick says, "Oh, not again." A fleet of bomber jet planes attack. "The dome should take care of it, but let's lay low anyway just in case." They lie on the ground, in the doorway and wait.

Rick says, "Twenty minutes have passed, please be silent as I try this again." He knocks the wall. It beeps. He shouts, "*Pistacia Terebinthus*," rubs the door in a circular motion, "*Marcellinus*," rubs the door in pattern of an anchor, "*White Rabbit Opp Bam*," then punches the wall. The wall slides sideways revealing a long passage down into the dark. "Bill, come quickly!" The wall beeps softly, and the beeps start getting faster. As they pass the door, the beeps sound almost continuous just before it stops beeping and slides shut behind them. The air is cool and humid. It is dark. In sudden exhaustion, they fall asleep.

Chapter

10

Rick and Bill don't know how much time has passed when they wake up. It is pitch black. Rick lights his bright electric lantern. It reveals a long sandstone hallway, leading down a staircase. Parts of it are solid sandstone, and others are held together by rocks and bricks. There are shelf-like ledges in the walls, each about 14 inches tall. Rick says, "Welcome to *The Dungeons of Britnoitula*. Over a thousand years ago, this was a secret ancient mass grave, called a catacomb. They were sometimes also used as a hideout. And it did not end with Constantine, as many are being taught. Not all agreed with the Emperor's particular form of faith. Many of the earliest protestants in the medieval era went into hiding and were forgotten by history."

"Sounds a lot like what's happening now with John Adramalech Balor."

"Yep. And we are now in the very same place they hid, one of their places, that is."

"It doesn't smell quite as bad as I've heard."

"All of the bodies were stolen centuries ago by warlocks, pirates and other vandals. We have also used our inventions to improve the environment, oxygen generators and the like. It was much worse when they had to use torches for lighting, as the smoke would use up much of the breathing air. As we have learned from the art on the walls, many learned to find their way around in the dark to conserve torch fuel and oxygen. The ancient excavators had shafts for breathing air, and letting in small amounts of natural light, but they clogged up a long time ago. That's probably one reason it got abandoned. We've also sealed the ground with the barrier field, which keeps out floods from the rising tides, and also protects us from attack."

"We somewhere in Rome?"

"We're far from Rome, but they started to explore other locations to build catacombs once the Romans were onto them. Obviously, we're under an island. I can't tell you where it is, though."

As they descend deeper, there is lots of intricate ancient artwork on the walls, mostly depicting Biblical scenes, and some occasional Greek mythology characters. Bill asks, "Did people really come down here to paint? There surely is a lot of art work on the walls."

"In ancient days many went into hiding, and I

imagine some were shut in for a long, long time. They found living in these tombs more tolerable than giving in to the Romans. When holed in for years, you just find things to do, no matter how foolish they seem. Also, it's a way of telling their story in a way that can be understood by people that didn't speak their language." Rick points to a painting showing Constantine in Babylonian attire, compared with Nebuchadnezzar as if it were a parody of the story from the book of *Daniel* about Shadrach, Mishach and Abednego. It shows three surviving being cast into a lake of fire by the Emperor. "Constantine supposedly legalized Christian faith in Rome, while continuing to grow the Empire of Empires, but you can see that some still had a reason to go on the run. And no, these outlaw fallout shelters, and the civil oppression that made them necessary, didn't end with Martin Luther. Just ask some of the Anabaptists from Germany, many who hid here." He points to another illustration on the wall.

"Kinda like what's happening right now with John Adramalech Balor?"

"Already told ya, but yep, more of the same. If we

did not have this *Atlantian Technology* thing from Nathan's notes, I don't know how we would survive here. Yet long ago, some really have, with not even a flashlight."

"Rick, you keep mentioning *Atlantian Technology*?"

"I consider our discovery of it a miracle. There are many inventions that we are still working on, and we just never know what we'll discover next."

The walk continues down a hallway, which looks like it's completely covered in bricks. Rick says, "The bricks and mortar are to seal the dead bodies behind them. It made the place quite a bit more inhabitable. The halls form a vast labyrinth. Stairs lead down, and another long walk through another level of maze. Rick leads the way through with a map on his laptop.

At the fifth floor down, they find a room that has a brightly glowing, tall, arch-like doorway in the middle of the room. A wire is connected to the magical-looking archway, and runs to a hole in the brick wall. Walking around the archway, it is like a flat pane. Looking into it, it seems to pulse in bright color. After looking for about forty seconds, Bill's eyes get used to it, and can see, as though through a holographic TV, what looks like the hallway of a fancy modern office building. There is also a digital calendar-clock on the cave wall.

Bill says, "I hope we have some kind of bathroom here, or I might have to desecrate the floor."

"No problem, follow me." Rick walks into the archway. Bill walks around the archway, and sees that Rick is no longer anywhere to be found in the room. When Bill gets back to the front of the archway, Rick looks like a character on the video screen.

Rick appears to be shouting, but Bill can't hear anything. Rick stares and beckons.

Bill, unsure of what else to do, walks into the archway. His body feels a tingle as he touches the screen, then he feels instantly forced through it.

Now, the air is much fresher. Elegant chandeliers light the polished wood and marble hall. Bill and Rick are standing side by side. Behind them is an archway similar to the one Bill just touched, and it depicts the dimly lit cave room they were in before. They enter a room. It has a window. It shows a blue sky, with thin cirrus clouds, and a sun about half size.

Bill says, "Now this is impossible. Is this VR?"

"No, it's real created space. By bending the space-time continuum, we inserted another three dimensional space, a micro-universe, all contained within that archway pane you saw in the center of that cave room. You said you needed a bathroom? Probably a good time for a shower too." Rick shows Bill to it. It's just like any other in the modern world.

After a refreshing cleanup, Bill says, "All the comforts of above-ground living?"

"Yea, though there is an interesting side effect. Time dilation multiple of twelve. For each minute you are here, twelve go by in normal space. For this reason, I've been trying to do more studying in the caves to conserve the passing of time. After all, we've only got five years left."

"Five years left for what?"

"The Seventh Year."

"Seventh year of what?"

"It was two years ago, that many disappeared. It is said that in the seventh year it may happen one more time, or they may come back and overthrow the Beast. While waiting for them, and their warring angels to come, we do all that we can to undermine the Beast. In the beginning the youthful allure of the forbidden is the only reason I liked computer hacking, but it grew on me to become a life-long passion. He points to and winks at a large photo of Richard Stallman on his wall. "Strangely, this self-proclaimed atheist seemed to have a gift of prophecy. Of course, the vast treasure-house of GPL software was not allowed on the internet censored by the John Adramalech Balor regime. It is becoming very popular again over our new network that just launched. We tend to be quick here, due to the time dilation. A whole day of the world goes by in two hours here. In fact, I usually sleep in the cave room. Although it's much more comfortable here, I rarely sleep here unless I'm sick. It's because a night of sleep here sacrifices over half a week of real time. Let's go now, I'll show you a quick look at the lab."

Rick leads bill to another room down the hall. It is a huge room with lots of scientific equipment. Rick says, "The invention of the Bamboo Router took place in this very room. However, most of the research and thinking took place back in the caves, again, to save time. We will soon relocate this lab into the caves, now that we have enough space dug out. Now one more stop on our sight-seeing tour." They exit the building. "Yea, it's quite a beautiful mountain and lake, what a shame that we can't pass the time here hiking and swimming, because, we would be passing too much time. Unlike the world above, we have access to plentiful clean water."

"Would be a great way to get out of the tribulation quicker, don't you think? Just hang out for five months, and it's all over."

"Yes, but we are also in a race against time to inform the world, which we are under prophetic obligation to do, as not to hide the light under a bushel. And, we also have to watch what happens to the catacomb that this is contained within. They keep bombing it. We have to make sure the defenses are still working. Anyway, it's been almost two hours according to your watch, so we'll return to the cave now."

They march, almost running, to the portal, walk into it, and are now back in the cave room. The clock on the wall shows that it's 23 hours and 12 minutes later. Rick shows an internet time check on his laptop, and proves that the clock is accurate.

Bill turns a knob on a device hidden in the brick wall that looks like a vent and says, "We also started to adapt our technology to make the caves a bit more comfortable." Air almost as clean as in the office building flows through the vent. "Next, I'll show you how we get our water and electricity here."

The journey down the mazes continues another five stories down. There are stalagmites dripping from the tops of the halls, as well as the occasional rat, bat, and mouse passing by. Bill says, "This looks just like the dungeons in an adventure game."

"These ancient structures are probably where they got the idea. Now here is where we produce our electricity."

They arrive in a huge cavernous room, with a large barrel hole in the center, with glowing coils. Bill says, "Nuclear reactor?"

"Close, but not quite. You've heard of thermonuclear fission and fusion, but this is different. This is *Direct Atomic Rectification*. You've excelled at physics, you know all about E equals M C squared, right?"

"Of course."

"This converts matter, almost any matter, directly into electricity. No heat, no waste, and almost no risk. And yes, I said," pointing to a pipe that's pouring in what looks like sewage, "almost any matter. What you dropped in that toilet is actually feeding our power grid."

"I can't smell it."

"Of course not. The matter is completely annihilated. Right over there, is an oxygen generation system, just like the kind used on nuclear submarines. We can also create other kinds of matter, by the way."

Another thirty floors down they descend through hallway mazes. They reach a room with a big hole in it, and it has about twenty electric water pumps. Bill says, "This is our supply of water, most of it is unused and goes into the lake inside the created space. Even if we couldn't go there, this prevents the dungeons from flooding."

They look around at more artwork on the walls. The paintings are quite intricate, and seem ahead of their time. There's plenty of what you might call ancient science fiction; Or is it fiction?

In a large vault there appears a painting over fifteen feet tall and thirty feet wide. It depicts ocean water, and a domed city underneath, with many tall buildings, antenna towers, and bright electronic-looking lighting. There are four young men standing at the front of the city, wearing glowing translucent space-age-modern-looking shorts and shirts. Under it is written in Greek, which Rick translates on his laptop, "We heard of this lost technology by prophecy. We had not the means to build it. One day a remnant of a far off future generation, in the third millennium of our Lord, will discover it, according to our dreams. And they shall raise up an unexpected challenge to the *Great Seven-Headed Hydra of Blasphemies*, the *Scarlet Whore*, and the *False Prophet*. They shall come to this very dungeon in the deep of this *island of the dead* when the *Antichrist Beast* is at the peak of his power, in the midpoint of *The Tribulation*. From that day shall remain one thousand two hundred ninety days until the final confrontation."

On another wall in this vault there is a painting showing a girl lain in a coffin, with his family standing around with lit candles. A white cloth is over the girl's body's eyes. A well dressed man with long gray curly hair points a finger on his right hand upward, smiling, right eye closed, the left looking up. His left hand is held flat and over the coffin, like a "stop" or "don't" gesture. In the cloudy sky background, there is an image of the same little girl, faint and barely noticeable. Everyone else's eyes are looking up at the image, and cone beams of golden light bear down on each of them from the image. A broken chain appears placed on the girl's body's chest.

Chapter

11

In the next room, Bill and Rick meet Melissa. Carrying a laptop, she says, "Now that you've proven yourself ready, Bill, I'd like to share with you an experience that I had the day after I got left out of the rapture." She starts reading from her journal file on her laptop:

"As I wake, and head into the bathroom, I am suddenly horrified beyond measure by my own reflection. It was a greater terror than that of being cut from the rapture, which was truly horrific indeed. I screamed and fell to the ground, for I saw my own pointing index finger with the Bible in the other hand being pointed squarely back at my eyes. I heard my own screaming voice in my own face, as if I was my daughter Tabitha, and my abusive preaching blasted from my mouth. It was a very highly detailed role-reversal flashback, and I experienced a triple-portion of all the terror and despair that my daughter went through as I was telling her that most of her friends at school would probably spend eternity in the lake of fire. Next, I floated away from my body again, all the usual things they say about how it happens. I really thought it was over for me, like, OK., so I'm gonna go to you-know-where, no more dangling and just cut to the chase and get it over with please. I found myself separated not only from space, but time. I was taken up into the spirit and thrust back to the time of the *Archdaemon Nimrod*. I saw the *Tower of Babel*, and another archdaemon floated over it, and his name is *Ba'al Re'Thoth*. There was also a human king that ruled in ancient Mesopotamia named Nimrod. He was also the great grandson of Noah from the Ark. The archdaemon that had his same name, along with *Ba'al Re'Thoth*, possessed Nimrod to rebel against God, and by this consortium with daemons did Nimrod craft a magick arrow that could pierce the *vital dynamic link between heaven and earth*. He had sought to inflict a wound on the *astral plane firmament* that would make it impossible to ever again speak between the worlds. If the attack had succeeded, the sun, moon, and stars would all go dark in an instant, and our universe and all that is in it would be thrust into the dimension called *Outer Darkness* for all eternity. The Lord showed me that there was another tower, just a diagonal dimension away next to the *Tower of Babel*, that nobody on earth has ever seen or heard of before. It was very similar to the *Tower of Babel*, but had no physical presence. The Spirit told me the tower can not be named, but represented an evil kingdom, unknown to any in the world, in an antimatter galaxy, in the image of *Babylon*, and was called *Embabylon*. It appeared at the instant that infernal magick arrow was aimed from the bow at the summit of *Babel's Tower*. The arrow bounced off the tip of this tower, and as it fell to the ground the *spell of division* fell upon those who dwell on the earth. And I was told, this other tower had averted what Nimrod had attempted, but allowed another archdaemon to come into the world, and his name is *Adramalech*. And I heard of the Spirit that although Satan controls each of these towers and their respective kingdoms, *Babylon* and *Embabylon*, it is in the clashing between them that the light of the Lord must pierce through to victory in the end."

Rick and Bill listen well, and Melissa continues her story. "I was then taken to the year 1986, in Asheville, North Carolina. I saw an occult ritual where *Ba'al Re'Thoth* himself was being summoned for the first time since the days of Nimrod, by some college kids studying mystical practices, but didn't know what they were doing. Some of the teachers did know what they were doing, at least somewhat. *Ba'al Re'Thoth* and the daemons accompanying him are fought by a legion of warring angels, and I saw the *fulcrum shard of light* that pierced *Ba'al Re'Thoth's* skull. The warring angel captain that bore the *fulcrum shard of light* says, as *Ba'al Re'Thoth* lay down for the count, *'Ba'al Re'Thoth*, by Yeshua, thou shalt be bound 'till the end of aeons, and thy servant daemons may no longer harm any of mankind with their poisons nor stings from the daemons' talons, and any deception they conjure up be made so harmless as to be transformed as unto a catharsis and healing by our Lord. The people will be granted the very heavenly gifts that your servant daemons have offered as bait to deceive. What was once called too good to be true, will come to pass. The very things your servant daemons offered as false hopes, the same will be fulfilled by the grand secret miraculous grace of our Lord Yeshua. No longer will the devil have the upper hand in the astral plane, and the *vital dynamic link between heaven and earth* will be restored. Satan did not create these powers you've been ruling, he was only allowed to think he did. For the devil does not create.' The warring angel captain took some magical-looking crystals out of *Ba'al Re'Thoth*'s pockets. He throws the crystals up to the sky, and they explode in lights of many colors like intense fireworks, and I saw that those crystals that the *Archdaemon Ba'al Re'Thoth* held for thousands of years were filled with the *secret powers of Heaven* and the essence of divine love. The veil between heaven and earth became thinner as the crystals reunited with the *astral plane firmament.* The warring angel captain says, 'Now we shall take the very thing that you have orchestrated to defeat the Lord, and use it for His ultimate purpose, and expose and defeat the other side of the twofold daemonic plot. Prince of *Babylon*, you are now a mere slave. *Embabylon*, in due time, is next in line to fall.' *Ba'al Re'Thoth* chuckled at the warring angel captain, 'But don't you know that the minister that called you down to defeat me had a bit of *Adramalech* in him? He does take after the Letter to the tee, after all.' The captain replied, 'Yea, but his heart is in the right place, for he never betrayed what he knew. He will understand this great accomplishment when the time is right.' The archdaemon murmurs in a soft but distinctly hangry growl, 'I can't believe what I'm seeing happen. The prayers of a fundamentalist Christian preacher helping to accomplish real universalism, what the fuck?' The warring angel captain says, 'The Lord does work in mysterious ways. He is doing exceedingly abundantly above and beyond what the minister could ask or think, and for this we are exceedingly glad. Now we shall take you to *Outer Darkness, Ba'al Re'Thoth,* your chains locked tightly around every nerve and vein of you indeed, that all the witchcraft in the world can never conjure thee up again. Oh how you were lured to this town, in hopes of taking it over, it was your trap from the get-go.' The warring angel captain pulls the *fulcrum shard of light* from *Ba'al Re'Thoth's* skull. *Ba'al Re'Thoth* screams, fading into the void, 'Mwha! *Adramalech* will see to it that *Embabylon* will rise! It'll destroy heaven and earth!' I was then taken to our present time. I was shown the stump of the hewn-down tree in the Bible prophet *Daniel's* vision; the very tree that once shown Yahweh's grace and anointing to Nebuchadnezzar himself. What looked like giant knotweed was growing through the stump, forming an image like the snakes of a medusa's hair, with clusters of thorns and heart shaped leaves. The bush was taller than the original tree, and was as wide as it was tall. And the thorns spewed tiny poison darts of fire. The Spirit said, 'this is the rising of *Embabylon*, which at this moment revives all the oppressions and abominations of *Babylon*, even to surpass them. The roots of this knotweed will go deep, even beyond the core of the earth' The plant had no physical existence, but brought about the growth of a great dark principality and power that is deceiving the very elect. 'Chosen people forgot what they were chosen for. Spiritual warfarers forgot what they were supposed to be fighting for. *Babylon* had rebelled against the Lord for other gods, but *Embabylon* now turns the Lord Himself into a creepy thing and a hateful bird worse than all the other gods. Still in the unseen, each kingdom, tree and tower, judges and fights with the other, *Babylon* and *Embabylon*, the legacy of the *Archdaemon Ba'al Re'Thoth* clasheth with that of the *Archdaemon Adramalech*, the *Tower of Babel* with its twin tower that can not be named; yet they are both likewise at this present time forms of godliness weighed and surely wanting.'"

Chapter

12

A rat scurries by. Melissa flinches away. Bill says, "Afraid of a little rrrAT, Melissa?"

Rick says, "They say if you get bit by a rat you'd better get to a hospital. You might get rabies. It could kill you."

Melissa says, "I can't go to the hospital. *Nurse Hatchette* and *Doctor Heddchoptophe* would have their way with me. Don't you remember?"

A faint sound of many footsteps is heard. Bill says, "Isn't this just like an adventure game dungeon? You never know when some kind of daemon is about to sneak up on you. Do you hear that, Rick?"

"It's the movers. Didn't I tell you before? They are rebuilding the lab in the caves."

The crew is passing by the hall, and Rick comes out and offers them some refreshments. One of the guys carrying the equipment shows an object that looks like a handheld mirror, "Remote viewing glass. We can see and hear what's happening anywhere."

The mirror-like apparatus shows a crowd of people somewhere on the west shore of Canada. They are celebrating and singing praises. A fiery mushroom cloud is overhead, about to incinerate them all alive.

This explosion is not from a human-made nuclear bomb, but sent from one of the *seven vials* of wrath, and they know it. The people about to be blown up continue to cheer, even at their own imminent divine wrath execution. They shout with excitement as they go up in flames, burned down to ash with not a trace of solid bone, "Nought is burned but the chains that bound us!"

Bill says, "I'd ask why they would celebrate, but the way things are going, we already understand. Could just assume craft a millstone amulet and have fun in the ocean if it weren't for all those brutal stinging mutant flying scorpions and the *Wormwood Plague*. Maybe scientists will find a way to make the flying scorpions into a food, to replace our lost supply of shrimp; if they can remove the poison, would like to know what they would taste like."

"Not as sweet as devil's food cake, I bet."

"Hey Rick, lets take a look at what's happening in John Adramalech Balor's Lair!" He hands one of the looking glasses to Rick. It has joystick-like controls and keypad buttons, and a video line output.

Rick connects the looking glass to his laptop, and

starts the video recording application. He turns the
joysticks on the device, and it shows the world
overhead, as if viewing from a space shuttle. Then he
zooms into Battle Mountain, Nevada, then into the
Grove of the Peacock of Stone, then into a chamber
deep under it. John Adramalech Balor is seen in his
office, with the witch Tammy McLillith. In the corner
of the room is a large cardboard box, labelled "Fetii –
(black markerred out) Hospital."

Melissa says, "On the surface, the John
Adramalech Balor administration was always very pro-
life, what some called anti-choice. Apparently, this
administration has no problem with secret forced
abortions, since they make convenient sacrifices to the
Archdaemon Adramalech. I bet it often stinks in his
office. He keeps the fetii at room temperature so they
can ripen, as that's how the daemon Adramalech finds
them most tasty in the fires of the belly of the *Great
Peacock of Stone*. The secret forced abortions are
usually made to look like accidental miscarriages, and
documented accordingly. My cousin worked in the
very hospital these came from, and knows all about it.
Nobody dares to blow the whistle, knowing what

happens to anyone who dares to fight with any kind of health care professional today. The hospitals are still killing babies, just not at the request of the mothers anymore."

As seen in the remote looking glass, Tammy McLillith is drinking what looks like a glass of wine. As she finishes, it is refilled from the same bottle that was filled with the blood of the beheaded protester from the church. It pours too thickly to be wine; It is probably the very blood of that protester, who was beheaded for her testimony of the Word of God, on live TV. Tammy McLillith drinks half of the glass of blood, and John Adramalech Balor drinks the other half. They refill the glass from the bottle, and continue until the bottle is empty. They refill the bottle with a brew made from rotten onions, bat guano, and pickled quints, and drink it down as a chaser. They have to cover their mouths and noses to keep from puking it up, and almost choke on it, turning dizzy. They cast the empty bottle into a burning fireplace. The bottle shatters from the heat of the flame, and at the same moment Balor and McLillith clap their hands once, sharply. They both cackle, and their eyes turn all black for a split second,

and there is a flash of purple light filling the office.
They fall on the floor in romantic ecstasy, and cry
"Thank you, Satan!" repeatedly. John Adramalech
Balor writes in his Grimoire, "O, praise be to the Devil,
for He telleth me of where they are hiding. Now we
shall find them! They were right under our noses the
whole time, under that island that we've been using for
military practice. I'll write more later, but for now we
shall make haste. In joy to Our Lord Satan, John
Adramalech Balor."

John Adramalech Balor says with a smile, "OK.
McLillith, lets go for a plane ride! How fast you think
you can get to that island under a full head of steam?"

"Maybe three hours. You know we could always
have those bomber jet planes go nuquelar, right? Cause
a great cave-in, then a white-hot thermonuquelar
firestorm underneath and fry 'em if you know what I
mean."

"Yes, but all our bomb-bombs seem to be bouncing
off of an invisible force field dome over the island. I
have no idea what the dome is or how it works. The
military haven't found a way to break it, and as The
Devil has told me, I will need to be there in person for

my magick to work on it."

The device goes blank. The crew member says, "We're still working on it, it's not that reliable yet."

Rick says, "We'd better inform the defenses crew." He calls on his walkie-talkie, "Shields up! Shields up! Balor will be here in person in about two hours!"

The monitor on Rick's laptop shows the surface view of the island, and several guards step out and watch the sky, each carrying a staff with an orb at their tops. Bill says, "I saw something interesting while Balor was writing in his journal. Maybe we could zoom in on the video?"

Rick transfers the file from Bill's laptop, "You could try."

Bill zooms in on a page in the Grimoire. Handwritten, *"Omnibus system design notes:"* at the top, lots of technical babble. At the bottom of the page, it reads, *"Back door password: SunimraNivlac1611"*. Bill shows it to Rick, "Hey hacker, what do you think this means?"

"Wow. Worth a try, at least." Rick opens up a command prompt window on the laptop:

```
rick@britnoitula:~$ telnet 0110.0110.0110.onion.bamboo
```

While waiting for response, Rick says, "As I have found out by poking around, John Adramalech Balor's Omnibus System is built upon what used to be called *the Dark Web*. There was a time when *the Dark Web* was actually a useful way around the censorship that was starting to take place, until he found a way to shut it down; at least that's what he said on the news. He actually took it over for his own secret purposes."

After a few seconds, The terminal window reads:

```
could not locate: 0110.0110.0110.onion.bamboo
connection timed out
```

Rick says, "Oh, I forgot to turn off the firewall switch." He flips a tiny dip switch on the router, and tries again:

```
rick@britnoitula:~$ telnet 0110.0110.0110.onion.bamboo
Omnibus0x666 login: root
Password: SunimraNivlac1611
Greetings, Dr. John Adramalech Balor, D.D.
No time for games.  You have mail.
root@Omnibus0x666:
```

Rick says, "Really? I can't believe it!"

Bill says, "What?"

Rick reaches out his hand to Bill for a high-five, "We just hacked... the very *Mark of the* fucking *Beast*! Thank God we're not back in the 1970's, it would have been so much harder. We'd then have to do this with an old *Texas Instruments scientific calculator*."

"What can we do from here?"

"Perhaps take a look around the system."

```
root@Omnibus0x666:ls -a
Desktop      Downloads    Documents    Projects
BankAccounts              CreditProfiles
MedicalRecords            BibleStudy
CareerManagement          RetailPOS    BroadcastMedia
Apologetics ThoughtControl             OCSChipUpdates
ArchdaemonWorship         FivefoldOrderMagick
BlackMagick NewWorldOrder
NewAgeTriangulationStrategy.txt
GrimoireNotes.txt    Grimoire.pdf         Agenda21
GroveMap    GroveSecurity    OCS_Dev
OmnibusCivilStabilityManifesto    .KittyPorn  .Trash
```

Rick says, "Now that I'm in, let's explore these dungeons; that's what hackers do."

"Aren't we already in the *Dungeons of Britnoitula*?"

"You get the idea."

```
root@Omnibus0x666:cat GrimoireNotes.txt
```

Bill meows, "Rreow?"

"Command to spit out to the terminal the contents of a text file." Rick hits the Enter key, and text comes rolling off the cursor:

```
    There has been an unfortunate turn of events, oh
lord Satan.  My sacred diary has been lost, or more
likely, stolen.  I will try my best to recall all that I
have written.
```

P.S. I found a copy of my lost Grimoire on the internet. The thieves blasted it to the whole world. Damn Christ, my secrets, my secrets, my precious secrets!

P.S. I have successfully gentrified the internet, and most of the people who know my secrets are gone in the rapture. Next, what to do about the Bible. Ah, yes. It's coming to me now. Ah, yes lord Satan, the machine is almost ready. My Kingdom cometh soon.

Praise be to the Devil,

John Adramalech Balor

root@Omnibus0x666:cat NewAgeTriangulationStrategy.txt

It's simple. Classic problem reaction solution, bait and switch, and divide and conquer.

Step one: We put the parts of the true Gospel of Jesus Christ that we don't want people to know about into a trendy philosophical movement. For the sake of metaphor, let us compare it to a cauldron for cooking up a soup. Add a half cup of questionable statements, such as, gee, our Power of Darkness doesn't exist. Ha, ha, ha! A pinch of salt, a teaspoon of sugar, and of course, a half gallon of party feelgoodism. Throw in some condoms, spandex fetishes and a disco ball for good measure. Oh, what a ball. Hold the bowl carefully, and mix well with the handle of an old fashioned witches' broom.

Step two: We preach against that movement, shouting it down as a work of the devil. By doing this, we also, in a slight-of-hand way, just like throwing a baby out with the bathwater, attack the true Gospel of Jesus Christ. In particular, we attack **the parts of the true Gospel of Jesus Christ that we don't want people to know about**; we can even use the very zeal for the Gospel of Jesus Christ to do it!

Now, we've actually gotten a majority of Born Again Bible-believing Christians to believe that those parts of the true Gospel of Jesus Christ that we don't want them to know about are deceptions from the devil, the good old angel of light. We did it, and it worked! Now, whenever someone expresses those parts of the true Gospel of Jesus Christ that we don't want people to know about, or in any way stand up to our limited atonement thing, whether by predestination or chance, all just as well, we can say, with all the weight of legitimacy from every Bible college and church in the world, **"They are not Christians!!!"** **Whoo!!!** **Praise be to the Devil!**

Amen,

John Adramalech Balor.

root@Omnibus0x666:cat OmnibusCivilStabilityManifesto

*** Omnibus Civil Stability Manifesto ***

* Upgrade the use of the triangulation strategy to the extent where the parts of the true Gospel that we don't want people to know about are completely forgotten by the public. **Accomplished.**

* As much as possible, remove all traces of that information from the world. *Mandela Effect Machine* has been invented, and it works. **Accomplished.**

* Install technology to monitor everything everyone does, and if possible, even what they think, at all times, in an inescapable way. The last step to making this happen was abolishing the right to consent to medical treatment. In a bizarre turn of events, the mostly atheistic Psychiatric agenda that hated us for so long, has settled our differences, and helped make this happen. When I told them the well guarded secret that I really worship the Devil, they were suddenly eager to work with our plan. We united against our common enemy, ***spiritual freedom***. **Accomplished.**

Melissa says, "It's true, I remember watching the votes in *HR* and *Senate* on *CSPAN* for an omnibus reform package bill that overturned parts of *CFR42* and many other laws, a nearly unanimous yay by both parties. Now the government assigns us all primary care physicians, and if we don't see them at least once a year, and obey their every order, no matter what it is, it's just like what happened to my old friends who were dodging the *Viet Nam* War Draft long ago. In short, you'd better run like you-know-where. They started doing that even before John Adramalech Balor came to power. Also, only the first four minutes of that mandatory appointment resemble a traditional physical. The rest of the hour is a full-fledged interrogation about your lifestyle. What do you eat, what do you wear, what do you believe, where do you go to worship, what organizations are you a member of, who do you talk to, what do you read, how do you manage your money, and, no joke, what do you think about when you play with yourself?! I had been warned not to even skip a single meal for the purpose of prayer, or I'd be carted off as a suicide suspect. It's called fasting. It is in the Bible. At least, it was before John Adramalech Balor modified all our Bibles. I tend to talk as little as I can get away with when I go to the appointments, and I learned the need to do this the hard way. Of course, it's hard to imagine why the annual visits are so necessary with," pointing to her forehead, "these damn microchips watching our every move. And, you can't look for another doctor when things get too hairy. That is considered an illness now, *Doctor Shopping Disorder*. Even if you were allowed to seek a second opinion, which used to be considered a right when we were a free country, it wouldn't do much good. They share their information on *the Dark Web* and are all working for the same agenda."

Rick says, "I've been able to hack in to career management before, due to some covert contacts with a school liaison, which was my cousin's liaison in more ways than one, but this is the first time I've ever been root."

"What does that mean?"

"I can see everything in the system. I can even shut things down. Watch this!" He opens a side window showing a soap opera on TV.

```
root@Omnibus0x666:kill -9 RetailPOS
```

Two minutes later, the TV cuts to "Special Report." All over the world, the checkouts at all the stores are not working. They don't know why they are out, and don't know how long it will be before they can fix it.

```
root@Omnibus0x666:kill -9 BroadcastMedia
```

The TV window goes dark.

Bill says, "Won't we get caught?"

"They're already coming for us. Perhaps I should do this too, don't know if it will do any good."

```
root@Omnibus0x666:rm -fMedicalRecords/MelissaTerebinth/*
```

"What?"

"I just R-M-dash-fuh, I mean, permanently deleted, the information about Melissa that you oversaw in that grocery store, and more."

"Will this allow her to drive and go back to the stores?"

"Probably not, because the missing information on her vaccinations and annual checkups will be suspicious. I guess I better do this as well, so they can't trace my connection."

```
root@Omnibus0x666:shutdown -r now
System is rebooting. NOW!
Disconnecting all users
Connection Terminated
```

Another moving crew member is showing off an

invention, "It's an invisibility field. Not quite large enough for a car, but it could do a motorcycle."

Rick says, "Great idea. Since Balor is coming here, maybe we can go back to the mainland on those amphibious bikes I've got stashed. I bet me and Bill can break into Balor's lair." Rick and Bill grab the devices, which fit on their wrists, and try them out. They can't see each other. They take them off and reappear. "Oh, maybe not now. Look." The laptop monitor shows the view from the surface of the island. More bomber jet planes are storming the surface, and this time a bright flash of golden mushroom cloud light erupts from the surface of the island. The invisible dome manages to keep the blast out, but the ground still rumbles. A sound of toppling stones is heard from above.

Rick's walkie talkie rings, "Cave-in on the third level down. All paths are blocked. Some radiation is penetrating the dome." As seen on the laptop's monitor, the trees on the island burst into flames. "God help us all, I'm surrounded by hot air. The rocks around me are glowing red. I'm about t- Ahh-"

Rick replies, "About to what? . . ."

No answer.

The deep rumble from above grows to an echoing hum. From where they stand, it looks like it's starting to rain dust and rocks, and it sounds like thunder preceding a heavy downpour. Now there is a heavy downpour of dust and rocks. The stone floor beneath them feels like it's sinking. The walls appear to be climbing. Faster. Bill says, "Is this an elevator going down?"

"We'll be in free fall soon. Duck and put your helmet on and hope for the best."

Chapter

13

The surroundings, which look like a huge well shaft of natural granite stone, start to flow upward, faster and faster. As they descend deeper, the stones become more blue in color. Rick says, "These look like ringwoodite crystals!"

Bill can't feel his weight. He shouts, "Freefall!"

In twenty seconds, splash! The rock they are standing on hits the surface of an underground lake. They are quite fortunate that the rock floor had something soft to land on, but the force from hitting it is still enough to knock everyone down with really bad bruises. They get wet, as the rock floor goes under for a few seconds before it bobs up and floats. Rick pulls out a rapid-inflate lifeboat from his backpack and pushes the button. Rick and Bill get in, just as the rock they were standing on starts to sink again. Melissa and the movers are nowhere to be seen, as they are probably still up there in the cave floor from where they fell. Rick tries to make contact on the walkie talkie, "It's Rick. Melissa, anyone up there?"

There is no response but static.

Rick gets the remote view looking glass to work again. Bill and Rick watch John Balor in the grove.

The *Peacock of Stone* is lit up with its belly of fire. Balor opens the box of fetii and drops them one by one into the belly of fire, cackling.

The devil appears and addresses John Balor, "Greetings John Adramalech Balor! Aye granteth thee..." An ugly gray belt, with images of chains and bonds finely etched through it, appears in front of the Peacock of Stone, at John Balor's feet. *"The Girdle of Thought Control!"*

John Balor removes the belt he has on, and replaces it with the devil's gift, and shouts, "Praise The Devil!" More fetii from the box are trickled into the statue's belly.

The devil continues, "Aye granteth thee..." A breast plate appears, solid gray. *"The Breastplate of Conformity!"*

Balor wears it, "Thank you Satan!"

The devil continues, "Aye granteth thee..." Black boots appear with spikes and spurs. *"The Bhuuts ... of ... War!"*

Balor kicks off his shoes, laces up the boots, "Praise be to the Devil! Whoo!"

The devil continues, "Aye granteth thee..." A shield

appears, of the darkest black, blacker than black, such that the more light you shine on it the darker it gets.

"The Shield ... of ... Fear!"

Balor picks it up, "Glory to the Devil in the Highest!"

The devil continues, "Aye granteth thee..." A helmet appears. One half is white, the other black.

"The Helmet ... of ... Partialism!"

Balor puts it over his head with haste.

The devil continues, "Aye granteth thee..." A sword appears. It is studded with thorny clusters, and at the center of it the image of the eagle, dove, and sparrow in chains under the book. *"The Sword ... of ... The Letter!"*

The devil continues, "Aye granteth thee..." A gray stone disc on a chain appears, left half black, the other white. *"The Amulet of The Divisive!"*

Balor hastily puts it on his neck.

The devil continues, "Aye granteth thee..." A ring appears, dark black, as dark as the shield. *"The Ring ... of ... Zealotry!"*

Balor puts on the ring, and increases with enraged anticipation, "Whoo! Praise you Satan! We burn with anticipation of POWW-ARR!"

The devil continues, "And finally, aye granteth thee..." A wand appears, also dark black. *"The Wand ... of ... Exasperated Hate!"*

Balor picks it up in haste, "Whoo! And as it be not the Devil's will that all should come to redemption, but that many should perish, we scoff at the *full armor of God*! We shall have our revenge!" The flames in the belly of the *Peacock of Stone* go higher and higher. A crowd dressed in hooded robes cheer Balor on in diabolical triumphant screams, and chanting along to praises of the devil.

The looking glass goes out again.

Bill and Rick row the lifeboat with their hands while watching this, and continue for a few hours more. They reach the edge of this deep underground lake, and wander around a vast rocky ledge. Looking around for hours upon hours, finding nothing interesting, they fall asleep simultaneously from exhaustion.

Bill and Rick wake up, and continue looking around finding nothing interesting. Bill says, "We'd eventually starve here? At least unlike all the waters at the surface of the Earth, there's no mutant flying scorpions."

Rick says, "Maybe some fishing?"

"Miles under ground, I bet nothing's biting."

"Look, I just found a worm!"

"What's the harm?"

Rick pulls out some rope and a pole and a bent paper clip, and rigs them up. They get back in the lifeboat and wait all day for something to bite. At least it seemed like a day worth of time, as they have no reason to keep track of the sun far out of reach. Their equipment can tell the time of the day, but at this point they don't bother checking. The only light is from the equipment they are carrying. In a futile wait for something to happen, they fall asleep in the boat.

Bill is woken by the chill of cold water suddenly engulfing him. He climbs back into the boat, and rows it to a shore, Rick still asleep. All the edges of the lake look the same, but this time Bill notices a faint figure on the blue stone wall. He says to Rick, waking him up, "Look!"

Rick and Bill rub dust off a surface of the rock with their hands. There now appears an indentation in a strange image. At the center, a five-sided bright blue gemstone-like image, resembling a humanoid face, perhaps gray-alien-like but geometrically simple, like pentagons. It has two golden orange rocky 'eyes' and a larger golden orange rocky circular 'mouth', like when one forms their lips to blow out. Around it is a doughnut-like image (torus) in dark blue, with lightning bolts flowing around it. The electrical bolts appear to flow in a spiral formation around the torus.

An apparition wanders into the scene. He looks like a 15-year-old boy, with dark auburn hair, and glossy teal eyes that perfectly match the color of the gemstone-face on the wall.

Rick says, "He looks like a character I think I've read about in Nathan's notes, but I'm not sure."

The apparition has shiny blue shorts with stars on them, and on his forehead are faint fine lines in the same shape as the image on the rock wall. He is carrying a large golden key. In it's handle are three circular images, in vivid color. On the left side of the handle, it shows a dolphin under dark blue water. On the right is a rainbow over a river, with a mountain behind, so straight and long that the whole rainbow fits on the river from end to end. On the top of the key's handle is the Pleiades star cluster. The figure winks and smiles at Bill and Rick. It walks over to the image in the rock wall, and places the key into the indentation. The figure giggles mischievously. Bill whispers to Rick, "I wonder why he's giggling."

The figure giggles harder, "No worries, hihihi."

Rick says, "Ut-oh! I suddenly remember who this character is."

The part of the rock wall containing the strange image jumps out, like a door slamming open. A bright blue light is behind it, and glowing water comes blasting out! The surface level of the underground lake rises rapidly. Bill and Rick are fully submerged within a half second. It feels deeper very quickly. The apparition flies by, winks, and fades away. Bill, holding onto Rick, reaches up vigorously, swimming upward as fast as he can. The pressure of the water rising helps them go faster, perhaps too fast. Within twenty seconds, Bill can see the hole in the cavern that was the ledge that fell. Bill aims for the hole, frantically correcting course. Their upward speed is about 40 miles per hour. Bill and rick fly upward out of the hole they came through, barely missing the hard rocky edge. The room is kept dry by the pumps that move the water into the created space lake. Having a lot of upward momentum, they fly. The stone at the top of this room is rushing toward Bill's head. Whack!

Bill is now floating in midair, and sees himself, blood gushing out of his crushed skull. Rick is standing there, shaken up and somewhat stunned. Bill looks Rick in the eye and says, "Rick?"

There is no response. Bill figures out pretty quickly that he's out of his body. The apparition carrying the key appears again, grabs Bill and starts flying upward, passing through the stone as if it were thin air. Above the island Bill and the figure fly, and the bombs keep coming down from the planes. A few blasts from the bombs hit Bill, but he doesn't feel anything. The flight continues into deep space. Bill says, "Where we going?"

"You'll see. I'm *the Guardian of the Fountain of the Deep*. You've heard the story of Nathan Anthony Tobit, right?"

"Yes."

"He had met me by another name. You will soon meet him, and Christopher Joshua, and several others involved in our quest."

"Does this mean the story is almost over?"

"Far from it."

In what seemed like less than a minute, the journey flies by through *the Eye Of The Needle* gate in the *Pleiades star cluster* and they land in the crystal city behind it. The sky is dark. There are few dim stars.

An apparition of a short old wise man, formed of flowing diamonds, greets Bill, "The seven sisters which once brightened this place to unbelievable beauty have gone out. The next brightest star, *Atlas*, sighed, threw up her shoulders, and decided not to give her light." He points to a barely visible outline circle in the sky. "The brightest one is now *Hades*, which give about half of the light of Earth's moon. This lake which was once filled with joy and frolic," pointing to the water, "is now brimming with fear, and *shadow scorpions* fly over it. You can see, now, that Paradise is beyond the verge of going dark. The *Darkness* is already upon us, and may soon overtake us."

Bill says, "But we have plenty of other means of producing light to see by."

"Except that this *Darkness* is not merely a lack of

lights as you know them, but a dreadful loss, a gaping rip in the fabric of *the essence of all that is good and true*."

A young-looking man walks by, and waves at Bill.

The wise-man apparition continues, "Christoper Raphael Joshua, this is William MacDonald Charles. You two are chosen, and must be sent back on a quest. Prepare to meet the unexpected. Now don't be alarmed by the apparent contradiction that you are about to see here, for what I have cleansed ye shall not call unclean. We've no time for unprofitable and vain strivings about the law; we've got a war going on. Meet the Prophet *Samuel* and *the Witch of Endor*!"

Bill is in shock, seeing a "witch" in Heaven, asks, "What's going on here?"

The Witch of Endor says, "From the time when the prophet *Jonathan* partook of the forbidden honey dew, to when Christ told his disciples to pluck the ears of corn on the Sabbath, many mysterious ways indeed. I was just a trickster, and did not really believe in what I was conjuring up. When the ghost Samuel appeared, it scared the crap out of me. I knew that only Yahweh Himself could have done this! I suddenly knew He was totally real. Saul was given over to judgment by death, and the fall of Israel was foretold, but this also came with an early revelation of the greater grace of the beyond. Samuel assured Saul that he and his family would be with him the next day. As I repented before the Lord Yahweh, and comforted Saul with dinner and prayer for mercy, I planned to burn all my collected astral knowledge. Yahweh's hand had stopped me. He said, 'we've got a war going on, with an enemy that would make the Philistines seem like nothing. We will need all the power we can get our hands on. Someone that is coming to the world in the future, named Yeshua, whom I shall call My only begotten Son, will want to see these notes.' I hid them under a certain tree, as He had directed me. 'He's gonna be raising the dead more than any other necromancer that had ever lived, or ever will. Not mere shades, but some alive again in the flesh, even Himself. And, spirits will even be recallable without any kind of ob, even when no remains of their bodies exist at all.' And, did you know? Endor was another name for the town of Galilee."

Two young guys walk by, both wearing white mesh shirts. One of them is wearing shiny blue shorts with the name "Noah" on one side, and a stick-figure image of a sail boat on the other. The other has silver shorts of a nearly identical texture but plain.

The Witch of Endor says, "I think I'll let Noah here explain why we don't see people being brought back all the time."

Noah looks the other young guy in the eye, tickles his shoulder with one hand, and side of his shorts with the other, and says, "Why don't you give the answer, Joshuabuddydrownd! Hihihi!"

Joshua tickles Noah back and says, "Caught in an undertow, I just fought it too hard, winded and stunned, my arms came to a standstill, and I was just awake enough to enjoy the perishing."

"That really turn you on? Wanted to go through it again, din't ya!"

"Yer angel-boy-teenager-friend-in-a-bathing-suit party all the time in the lake over there," pointing to the lake that has the *shadow-scorpions* flying and crawling on it.

"Now you got me jealous, three more days than me playing in the water with the angels."

"It went by fast. I was quite surprised at how

sensual it was, now that's all gone, as we know, when came that awful night when the seven candles and the seven suns went dark. Anyway, you don't see the Lazarus thing very often because we don't like being thrust back into the mortal world against our will. Many occult mediums were the equivalent of the prank late night doorbell ringer. Just ask that lady who killed herself after her husband brought her back to life in the flesh, although good luck getting her to want to talk about it."

The Witch of Endor continues, "Israel and its law foundation must face its downfall, both by enemies and by collapse under its own weight, in order to make Yeshua's coming possible. Later, long after my passing away from *Malkuth*, I saw that when Yeshua was crucified, the Spirit of the Lord had left that golden box, and it wasn't long before a terrible evil moved into it. Warlocks carried it to a secret chamber. People mysteriously got sick from being near what's been rumored its location. Now, it would be ridiculous to claim that people got sick from being near the Holy Spirit, so some have speculated that something very evil must be in there. And it's true. Bill, you saw exactly what it was."

Samuel shows the *Menorah of Shalom* and says,
"The last of the flame of the *Candle of Philadelphia* has
gone out, quite a while ago. *Atlas* refuses to give her
light, and we are now only lit by *Hades*, and the more
distant stars are dimming and falling away. Madam,
show Bill and Chris what they need to know."

The Witch of Endor pulls out an orb, and says,
"Chris and Bill, enter this Orb. You will be able to talk
to each other, but no one inside the scene that it will
show you can hear or see you. What you need to know
must be shown, not told."

Chapter

14

The orb draws in Bill and Chris's vision, and they begin to experience what they see inside as though it were actually happening.

They find themselves in a hallway. The floors are made of gold, and the walls of jewels. People, mostly upper-middle-aged, and a few children under five, but nothing in-between, are laboring intensely washing the floors and walls. They pass by a man and woman working together, who sing while they scrub the floor wearing thick, formal, expensive-looking attire, *"Freedom from Sin by Slavery to God."*

Next, Bill is drawn into the minds of the two who are scrubbing the floor, and now knows the big picture here, what everyone here knows but can't talk about. This seems to be a form of Heaven built strictly according to the letter of the Bible; Actually, John Adramalech Balor's modified version of the Bible is more likely. "Worship God", you can't do anything else, can't say anything else, can't think or feel anything else. The trees were so uniform that they seemed unnatural, too straight, and their leaves would never flow with the wind. The rocks would align too perfectly, so one could not easily tell them apart from bricks. Clouds appeared as plain rectangles. The sky seemed to be lit constantly, in an uncomfortable glare like a really powerful cheap fluorescent light. Birds always flew in single file, and never danced in changing formations like they did before. Does anyone ever swim in the pond? Only very occasionally, in a boring way, and for a short time, barely enough to get themselves clean or cooled off from their labor. No playing.

The wandering through the vision in the orb continues. Artists, writers and musicians were forced to write nothing but worship-genre material. No modern scientists made it here at all. It was said that they all went to Hell because the Gospel was too simple for them to accept. Songs were extremely simple, pretty in a superficial way, such that they would be painful for a sophisticated mind to sit through. Any sophisticated art or higher energy entertainment was shunned, and was considered part of witchcraft and idolatry. They would say "it's entertaining allure distracts from the worship of God, and it's, therefore, of the world, and we must leave it behind." If it weren't for their thoughts and feelings being totally controlled, they would surely miss the things of the world, let alone the more jubilant and cosmically inclusive paradise many hoped for, which once was a reality before the seven suns and seven candles failed. There was no creativity, and there was no ambition. Furthermore, nobody here ever accomplishes anything whatsoever, for any unique human accomplishments were shunned as if they were sin. There was only what they called "being used of the Lord," to the condemnation of all else whatsoever, and this condemnation was the very foundation of their salvation. They were aware, yet lacked the ability to complain, or even want to, because they "gave their life, heart and mind to 'the Lord'" lock stock and barrel. To Bill, watching while still in a free mind, it really seemed more like: Yo! Hello; they sold their souls to the devil to get saved.

The very concepts of love and mercy were reduced to merely a withholding of punishment. People were forced to romanticize this mere leniency to the elect few in mandatory songs of worship. The thoughts of many mystics who thought the scriptures had deeper meanings were dismissed as "deception" and wishful thinking, and forgotten. *The Akashic Record*, which was also called *the Book of God's Remembrances, the Scroll of Zoe,* and *the Book of Life,* was destroyed. Something called "the Book of Life" was then made to take its place, but it was merely a small book containing a list of human names. The *book of the damned* was much bigger. All other knowledge in the original *Akasha,* which was really much more than a book, such that the universe could not contain it if it were, was gone.

People were constantly reminded that their personal savior is torturing the vast majority of eternal spirits of humankind in fire, forever and ever and ever and ever and ever and ever and ever and ever and ever and ever and... thrown away the key and all that. This permanent punishment clearly had no goal of correction, and was, by definition, and by every possible objective measure, outright abuse. They claimed that "because God is holy," He must do this obvious evil permanently, and make everyone call that action just and holy. They were also constantly reminded that many of those lost souls were actually far more innocent than themselves by every possible objective measure. Most who had died between age 8

and 35 were down in you-know-where. The few of
these that did get saved were instantly transformed to
something like the age of 35, and told to "leave behind
childish things." Infants were allowed to live as small
children, but once reaching about 5, they were instantly
turned to something like the age of 35.

The fun half of childhood did not exist. Nobody
developed any imagination. They were under law, in
the most meansomber sense possible. They had the
kind of surly maturity that only sees the bad side of the
young-people's-world, so it was shunned, as they
would explain, "for the safety of their souls." It wasn't
exactly Mosaic law as in the old testament, but it was
still do, think, and feel, exactly as you are supposed to,
or else. "Trust the Lord" actually meant to squirm,
cower and back down under the bossy pressure.
Nobody developed intelligence above IQ 75, as it was
exhorted that only God should ever do any thinking.
Having any original thought of your own whatsoever
was shunned as a sin. Even a good idea, this jealous
God would insist on calling evil just because it wasn't
His.

The Apostle Paul's scriptures about release from

the law (modified by Balor's machine) were understood as only a temporary release to give our souls just one last chance. One more strike and you're out was the hope of the Gospel.

The word "fun" was not in people's vocabulary at all. Anything that we think of as "fun" was called "sin." For example, from here, a 9-year-old's back yard birthday celebration, if people were allowed to remember such things at all, would not be considered innocent by these stuffy fear-driven holiness standards, and would have to be repented of just as if it were drug use or a bloody satanic worship ritual. This was explained as, "It was called innocent fun from a human standpoint, but it's an unnecessary activity not directly related to the faith, therefore it's sin." There was absolute zero sense of humor, for this was the eternal Kingdom, literally a monarchy, of the God of the letter, the God that hated the wink of the eye! The thought of even the possibility of creative innocence was shunned as a sin of deception. Any desire for anything that was not an immediate necessity for either survival or worshipping "the Lord" was condemned as sin.

"Holy" originally meant, among other things,

morally beautiful, heroic, trustworthy, and rooted and grounded in love. However, here, "holy" meant vindictively bossy, demanding and intolerant.

There was no friendship. There was no personable affection between anyone. People did not recognize each other, even their own children, if they made it in at all. People did not really talk to each other at all. Except for worshipping God, they were unable to say anything whatsoever. Their controlled minds made them not only accept but love and praise this situation, with obnoxiously simple and superficially pretty songs and slogans, which one could imagine being sung in a snide smirky fake smile. They would sing *"Isn't Jesus wonderful, isn't Jesus wonderful* (repeated forty times, in the exact same melody using only two notes)" as they watch billions burn in torment, some of them their family and friends, and, as they are constantly reminded, no more guilty than themselves of anything by every possible objective measure. They were constantly reminded that it was too late, too late, and nothing but too late to make any kind of difference for anything or anyone. This would surely bother any Christian of conscience; there would be weeping and gnashing of teeth in this Heaven. However, they were under mind control, and emotional paralysis, driven to celebrate this rather empty victory to the Lord's rescue mission, which was in the end downright puny in its power and reach.

As we wander, we hear two women working with mops and sponges on the streets of gold singing a song in glib callous tone, like any other expression that would ever be allowed or even possible here, under the mind control:

The thief on the cross is burning in Hell.

Yet the murderer is with us today.

For this is His justice,

And this is His mercy,

And except for our praises we shall have no say.

By the way, the Bible never said those lines until John Adramalech Balor added them to the book of *Romans* with his *Mandela Effect Machine.* One of these women was the mother of the Apostle Paul. The other was the mother of Judas Iscariot, but she does not remember that her own son ever existed, thanks to the mind control. Bill wishes he could speak to her, and thinks, "just imagine how she would feel if she knew!"

It was mandatory to sing that song in front of the *Three Crosses* image at least once a day. Whether by predestination, as some believed, or take-it-or-leave-it, as many believed, they were not allowed to know which of these theories twain was the case. The bottom line in the end were an excess of forgiveness to some, yet zero forgiveness to the others. This example of sheer partiality was enshrined as the very foundation of why anyone is here at all. Gee, why don't they just go ahead and make the point behind that symbol more obvious by flipping one of the crosses upside down?!

The streets were paved in gold, no doubt, and the walls were of jewels, but everyone had to labor washing them all the time, being "used of the Lord." They sing exactly what they're supposed to, think exactly what they're supposed to, and feel exactly what they're supposed to.

Many who had been through extreme tragedy did have the tears wiped from their eyes, no doubt, but in a way like unto having the tear ducts ripped out of their skulls. Rather than actually solving tragedies with miracles and truly graceful revelations, the "Lord" stripped the handful of souls that made it to this Heaven of the ability to care about anyone or anything at all. Everyone seemed like they had a lobotomy.

It was all about the *Straight and Narrow*, with no end to that narrowness. From Bill and Chris's vantage point, seeing this while their minds were still free, everything was so intolerably coldhearted that if it were not for the mind control, everyone would probably want to leave. This Heaven was an institution; hence, they'd sing "In our Father's house there are many rooms," and never "mansions." For the few that were saved were mere servants, as butlers and scullery maids who worked in a mansion that was someone else's property, the bossy rich man and king "God." And, of course, they were back to old fashioned gendered occupations, the women having most of the dirtier jobs. And they still sang, with a type of happiness that was forced, about being "used of the Lord," and it really meant being used, and used up, forever.

Since people always had to wear 1950's-like Sunday-best at all times, even when maintaining the outhouses, there was a lot of laundry to do. There were no machines, for electronics and other inventions were shunned as "that's a part of witchcraft." Everyone knew that Thomas Edison was down there, for he was a spiritualist heretic. For the creativity that made inventions possible came from people having original thoughts, what's called "thinking outside of the box", but, as was often exhorted, "The mind must never wander nor wonder, for all who wander or wonder will be lost."

This state of salvation was a bit like spending eternity in the frying pan for avoidance of the fire, something we just had to settle for, that is, just... accept. Just accept. You must accept. The very foundation of this Heaven was to glorify the outcome of everyone else going to you-know-where, and, of course, unconditionally surrendering your will to the God of that outcome. It was really to the point of worshipping that outcome, as if that outcome, Hell fire itself, were in and of itself the Christ.

'Twas the *Straight and Narrow* indeed, *Straight and Narrow* forever. Overly reverent. More buttoned down than the worst corporate office bored-room in the world, like in a company that can't keep any employee they would not want to fire. This weight of eternal glory was about as satisfying to the human heart as the proceedings of a debt collection case in court. For the ultimate prize was to hear of the "Lord", *"Well done, thy good and faithful slave!"* They've made it through their trial period to prove their one-way-street-loyalty, and now have the privilege to continue in servitude; for "being used" were all there is and ever will be, 'twas either this, or "be a slave to the devil," they were reminded often. To make one's own decisions was actually something to be feared! And forget all those romantic-looking paintings of angels by artists of the world; angels were about as cute and cuddley as the jail guards of Alcatraz.

This was eternity in the taste-not-touch-not, where even the ability to desire or imagine anything is restrained out of existence. It was quite a stark contrast to the free-spirited frolic Chris and the others had in Paradise just before John Adramalech Balor came to power on Earth, and shook down the stars of Heaven. Only the mundane ultra-conforming who were willing to hate all enjoyments were saved. It was not so magical! It was not so spiritual! Above all, mundane and unfree, except for, of course, those songs about *freedom from sin by slavery to God.*

Bill and Chris see further into the future, what seemed like a billion years later, although time was not really measured anymore. Like *the Parable of the Boiling Frog*, this form of Heaven collapses under its own weight into a *Completely Gravitation-Collapsed Singularity*, also known as a Black Hole. And, very dark is this Black Hole. Satan breaks out in triumphant cacklery, for the Hells were greatly enlarged, Heaven were burst into flames of nuclear Hell fire and laid to waste to nothingness; and exasperated hate, bondage, gruffness, grimness, sheer terror and above all, *Wrong Itself* were all in all forever and ever.

Just as he is about to be consumed by this Black Hole, Bill feels an arm behind him, pulling. He and Chris are now out of the orb, before Samuel and the *Witch of Endor*. She says, "Chris, listen behind thee, for I call a deep voice on your behalf, *the Still Small Light within the Core of the Dark*. Then, let the Holy Spirit confirm His reflected call." and stares into Chris's eyes.

Chris hears from behind, an intense whispering voice without even an astral body, "I know what you just saw within that orb. That is what shall become of

Paradise if you should fail on your quest."

Chapter

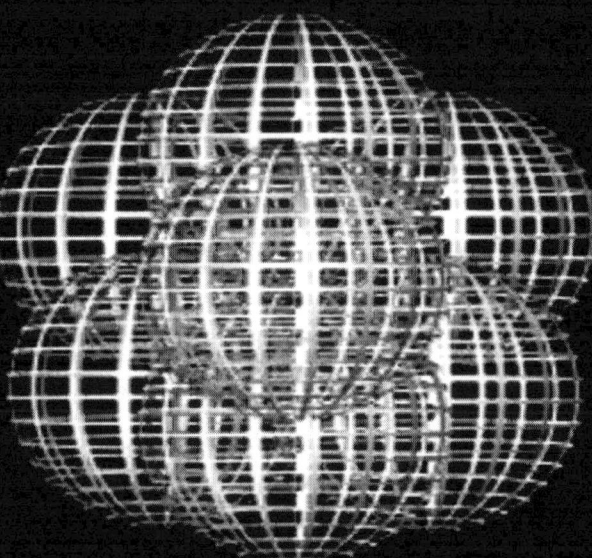

15

The wise-man apparition says, "I know what you have seen and heard. That is what's at stake here, on this greatest gamble. Now I shall show you a bit more." He escorts Bill and Chris to the throne room, and points to the stone table with the nine notches containing the *Girdle of Truth, the Breastplate of Righteousness, the Shoes of Peace, the Shield of Faith, the Helmet of Salvation, the Sword of the Spirit, the Amulet of Unity, the Ring of Wisdom, and the Wand of Unconditional Love.*

The *Amulet* on the stone table projects to a wall a message, very dim and barely visible even in the dark, "Remember them that are in bonds, as bound with them; and them which suffer adversity, as being yourselves also in the body."

The wise-man apparition gives Bill and Chris each a cloak, which appears to be made of many colored flowing crystals, "This is *the Cloak of Numbering.* Until your part in your mission is completed, you can not possibly die. When you return to *Malkuth*, you will not be able to see it, but it's there."

Bill asks, "*Malkuth?*"

Chris says, "What we call the mortal universe

plane, wherein Earth resides, from here. Since time is passing much more quickly than usual here now, it will be about five years later when you go back in. The seven years are almost over. We must make haste."

The wise-man apparition continues, "You will return now. Break into Balor's lair, and you will know what to do from there."

Bill is now back in his body. Rick is bandaging Bill's wounds. Chris is standing there. Rick is in shock, and says, "Bill, you were dead for five years. I just can't believe it. Somehow I just couldn't bring myself to bury you, and your body seemed to avoid any rot. Neither worm nor beetle came around, and I could not smell anything. And are you really back, here in the flesh, Christopher Raphael Joshua?"

"Yes, it is I. Bill will tell you about his journey, I'm sure. Now, we must get into Balor's lair, for Paradise is worse than lost if we don't succeed. Got those invisibility field bracelets and amphibious motorcycles ready?"

"Yes, but hopefully the radiation from the bombs didn't hurt them." Rick loads the security camera viewer on his laptop. The sky looks quiet. "Might be a good time to go, the bombers are at least taking a break."

Bill, Rick, and Chris take a long fast walk up the catacomb levels. Luckily, the cave-in blockage has been drilled through, and they pass by Melissa, who is doing all right on the third floor, where they are moving part of the invention lab.

As they reach the surface, Rick shows Bill and Chris to the amphibious motorcycles, gives them bracelets, and instruction printouts. Rick says, "I'll be staying here, someone has to be the general to the fort." He pulls out some more gear from a giant suitcase. "And I didn't forget, here are your helmets and pad armors. Wear them well. Good luck, or, better yet, I should say, God speed!"

Bill and Chris fist-bump Rick, wink, smile, then get on their bikes. They push the button on the bracelet to become invisible, and ride on the ocean. These bikes have very powerful motors and don't need any fuel. They run on *ambient zero-point electricity*, which is an unlimited source of energy hidden in the space time continuum, which can now be tapped thanks to the *Atlantian Technology* from Nathan's notes. It doesn't take long for the bikes to reach a speed of 1200 miles per hour on the water. Bill laughs, "We can't get a speeding ticket if they can't see us!"

"Hope we don't crash into an iceberg before we can see it!"

"I might have run over a shark."

"That's impossible. They are extinct now."

"Yea, but there seem to be plenty of monsters. Any idea where the Seven-Headed Hydra of Blasphemies may be? I'd love to give that monster a real hard tire rashing!"

"I don't think I want to know until I need to. It would probably blow seven streams of dragon fire at us if we ever crossed its path."

Once they reach land, the have to slow down somewhat to dodge traffic. Still, they take as much advantage of their fast bikes and invisibility as they can, often going between cars, over the breakdown lanes, and making jump-ramps out of the ditches.

Chris laughs as they pass by an orange "BUMP" sign that's been modified by a prankster. It reads, "BOMB!"

Bill says, "We better slow down, at seven hundred

fifty miles an hour that pothole might as well be a bomb."

"I see it, we can dodge it."

"We better dodge that!"

They are in the oncoming traffic lane, and a Dodge Ram is bearing down on them. They ride into the ditch to dodge the Dodge Ram, then back onto the road in a way that jumps their bikes 420 feet in the air, arcing over a half mile of traffic. The bikes make a perfect landing.

Chris says, "The only thing missing here is a Carpenters record and some helicopters!"

"I've got some Judas Priest CDs, that'll have to be good enough." The music sounds quite clear, since the electric motors in these bikes are almost silent. "Oh, look!"

A black helicopter flies overhead, armed with missiles.

"I thought nobody could see us!"

The helicopter follows their path for a few minutes, but flies away.

"Probably nothing to worry about there, nothing to do with us, just coincidence."

As traffic gets thinner after 9 PM, they can now ride somewhat smoothly at 520 miles per hour, and quickly reach the site of the *Grove of the Great Peacock of Stone*.

Bill says, "Since the bracelets can't be left with the bikes and on our wrists at the same time, we'll have to hide the bikes somehow."

"We could easily camouflage them in those cacti!"

Wearing thick gloves, Bill and Chris hide the bikes in the cacti, uprooting and overlapping some of them. The invisible bikes reappear as Bill and Chris step nine feet away from them, but would not be noticed behind the cacti.

Still invisible, Chris and Bill walk past all the warning signs. Images of skulls, owls and peacocks are everywhere. A sign reads, "Trespassers will be cast into the Lake Of Fire!" Another reads, "!esiR lliW nolybabmE" That's *"Embabylon Will Rise!"* backwards. Another depicts the seven-headed hydra with ten horns.

Chris and Bill pass by a shed where some half-bald redneck middle aged men are in drunken revelry. Chris says, "Borr-ring! Probably not worth dropping even a soffit or fascia here. Lets move on."

There is a man patrolling the path. Chris whispers, "We'd best hide behind that tree."

"Why? They can't see us."

"Shh!!! Maybe wizards can."

Bill and Chris quickly hide behind the tree until the guy patrolling the path is out of their line of sight.

They come to the Peacock statue, which is just resting, and there's nobody there. Out of curiosity that seems to be wearing off quickly, they look at the pipes that feed the fire in the belly. Bill feels not much more excitement from being here in person than reading about it in Chris's old notes. Really, his mind is disappointed after the manner of, "OK., please show me something I don't already know."

Chris says, "We're in the midst of the thriller. You're bored? Really? I think someone might have put a spell on you!"

"Self-contradictory but true. I'm not seeing anything yet that we don't already know, let alone any clue about what to do next. Did we come all this way for nothing?"

A young guy is walking by, whispering under his

breath, "I can't believe I got in, just can't wait to show it off at the frat party." He has a video camera hidden in his pocket, with a hole for the lens to see through.

A security officer walks up to the young man, and whispers "Trespasser" into a walkie talkie. Bill and Chris hide behind another tree. Three seconds later, a man in a hooded purple robe runs into the scene, and yells, "Eh, heh, heh, Aye baptize thee ... in," pointing at the young man in a magickal gesture, "FYE-ARR!"

A solid circle of fire appears and burns the young man alive, down to ash and bone within a tenth of a second. The man in the hooded robe cleans up with a witch's broom and dustpan. Chris whispers, "He's got magick, we better get away, maybe he can see us."

They quickly and quietly move on from the area, and find the entrance to John Adramalech Balor's secret office. They peruse the documents that Bill, Rick and Melissa saw through the remote viewing looking-glass. Not much there that they didn't already know. Bill says, "Now that we're here, do we know what to do?"

"I have no idea."

"Neither do I. I hope we haven't wasted our time. All this could be for nothing."

"But we're doing what the wise-man apparition said. He said we would know."

"I just hope that He knows what He's doing, if you know what I mean."

Bill and Chris both get down on their knees, and Chris leads, "OK., Yeshua, Now what?!"

Chris says, "Behind this door!" He leads Bill to a door half way down the hall.

Opening this door reveals a machine, which fills the whole room. It has many glowing coils of what look like electromagnetic windings. They form a pattern like three sixes, the tail parts of them conjoined at the center. They slowly spin inside another coil in the shape of a doughnut. Bill says, "I bet this is the *Mandela Effect Machine*! Let's pull the plug!"

Bill can suddenly see Chris, and himself.

Chris says, "Something wrong with the invisibility bracelets? Or maybe they don't work too close to this machine?"

"Ut-oh!"

"We better get out of here fast!"

A man carrying two Glock Machine Pistols comes barging in and yells, "Stop, I'll shoot!" and immediately fires a spray of forty bullets into the foreheads, chests and necks of Chris and Bill, in roughly equal portion. The bullets bounce off their skin. Images of cloaks appear to glow in white on Chris and Bill, pulsing with each hit from a bullet.

Bill finds the power cord to the *Mandela Effect Machine* and rips it out of the wall, pulls out a knife from his pocket and cuts the wire. He feels a jolt vibration from his left pocket, which has a miniature Bible in it.

The gunman seems a bit shocked, but maintains an almost mechanical level of composure, and whispers something into his walkie talkie. The gunman pulls a Bible out of his pocket, and opens it and flinches as he looks at the verses. Within one second, four purple hooded wizards appear around Bill and Chris and immediately cast, very rapidly, "Aye baptize thee in FYE-ARR!"

Chris and Bill are engulfed in flames. As if it were not happening, it doesn't hurt. The cloaks glow again.

The wizards try again, and cast even louder, "**Aye baptize thee in FYE-ARR!!!**"

The flames are seven times hotter, three times

higher, almost touching the ceiling of the office.

The cloaks glow, and Chris and Bill can't even feel the heat.

The wizards run, murmuring, "Ut-oh, they've got some kind of strange magic."

Bill says, "That was a close one."

Chris says, "Ut-oh!"

John Adramalech Balor appears instantly in front of Bill and Chris, in a flash of blindingly bright dark black light, (or is it *an intense flash of darkness*?), wielding his staff, and screams, "***Aye baptize thee in HELL FYE-ARR!!!***"

The flames go higher and higher. Chris and Bill are not hurt. The ceiling is now starting to burn. Balor says, "Oh, no, not again. **CHRISTOPHER J-**! hic hic At least I knew enough to install fire extinguishers this time."

Balor runs to a panel, in the hallway just outside this machine room, labeled "**Fire Extinguisher**" in bright red letters. He opens it. Opening the fire extinguisher panel reveals a can of kerosene. He screams "**Oh no, what the fu-!**" and runs for the exit door.

Bill says, "We got nothing to lose in the building, but they do. I'd not mind letting that machine burn up before they can try to fix it. What are we waiting for? **Get him!**" Bill and Chris begin to chase after Balor, but give up and pop out the nearest exit they can find, which is on the opposite bank of the river from the *Great Peacock of Stone*, which is now ablaze in the belly. Balor and several of his wizards are just finishing up a ritual. A great seven headed red dragon, with diadems on each head, comes flying by, lands on the river, and Balor converses with the dragon in an unknown language. Bill says, "This is *the Seven-headed Hydra of Blasphemies*. I recognize the messages on the foreheads. Only he's now become a fire-breathing dragon!"

The office building goes up in flames.

Balor says, "Oh well. I lost my notes again, but The Devil remembers it all anyway, and, the last spell I'll ever need to cast hath been consummated!"

The dragon splashes water from the river onto the building, putting out the fire. Balor bows to the dragon, "Thanks," and continues to converse with the dragon in unknown languages.

The sound of a girl screaming is heard from the statue. Chris says, "Bill, that's Clarissa Methodiste. Balor murdered her and stole her soul."

Since Balor has his eyes fixed upon the seven-headed dragon in conversation, and the evil wizards are taking a coffee break, Chris decides it's a good time to swim across the river. Bill says, "I'll wait here. I'm not going anywhere near that thing."

Chris turns off the valves in the statue, picks up a bucket and pours water from the river into the statue's belly, putting out the fire. Balor starts to turn his head toward the statue. Chris quickly ducks under the side of the statue opposite to where Balor is standing. He can hear Clarissa, the spirit of Mark's daughter."

Balor says, "Hmm… probably some of the water splashed by the dragon got in. At least the spell was completed just in the nick of time," and turns his head back to the dragon.

Chris reaches into the belly of the Adramalech statue and pulls out a black obsidian orb. Carrying it, he jumps in the river and swims back to where Bill is standing. Clarissa is heard crying from within the orb.

As the dragon is about to take off flying, an

apparition that looks like a 9-year-old boy angel
appears and flies in front of it, waving a "stop" gesture.

Chris says, "It's Mikey, the untimely departed
friend of one of our traveling companions."

Bill says, "He wasn't mentioned in the journal."

"Joey's friend. And Joey really shocked his dad.
When Joey found out how his friend died, he already
knew through a dream, and actually thought it was
funny."

Balor chuckles, "So this is what the enemy
Yahweh, Yeshua, Christ, whatever, what's the
difference, sends, to fight against our great seven
headed dragon, a wee buddy hug . . . hihihi oh, don't
make me laugh too hard, our victory will be so easy;
Praise the Devil! Dragon," and converses with the
dragon in unknown languages.

The seven heads of the dragon surround Mikey in a
circle, and blow fire. Mikey stares back defiantly at
each of the seven heads. The fire was not affecting
Mikey at all. All seven heads bite, and bite hard
through his neck. The teeth just pass through, and
Mikey is unharmed as if the teeth were not even there.
John Adramalech Balor is now watching with a

shocked and puzzled look plastered all over his face.
He mumbles, "That's just not possible. It must be some
kind of trick. Oh no."

Mikey ducks under the river water, and flies up
laughing.

Balor says, "Oh I see, too wet to burn. OK.,
dragon," and converses with the dragon in unknown
language.

The dragon's seven heads blow fire into the water,
and it starts to boil.

Mikey sees a *Pistacia Terebinthus* shrub near the
edge of the river. He flies over to it while the dragon is
not looking, and picks some seeds from it. From the
twigs and stems he forms a sling shot. He flies back
out to face the dragon, over the boiling river, and lobs
the seeds into all fourteen of the seven-headed-dragon's
eyes. The dragon is stunned. Chris says, "The dragon
is headed for a real deep baptism if you know what I
mean."

The dragon loses consciousness before the river is
cool enough to touch without burning off a hand. John
Adramalech Balor and several of his wizards try to pull
the dragon out of the river, but the monster is just way

too heavy. Huge bubbles filled with thick black smoke stinking of sulfur dioxide, flowing up from each of the dragon's heads, rise from the river even as it cools.

A vast army of huge, tough warrior-like apparitions flock in from the clouds. Chris smiles brightly, looks John Adramalech Balor squarely in the eyes, and says, **"John Adramalech Balor, You have been weighed and found wanting. Your reign of terror has come to an end."**

The warring angels grab John Adramalech Balor, the witch McLillith, and several of their accompanying wizards by their throats. A captain of the warring angels speaks, "Amen, Christopher Joshua. Now, John Adramalech Balor, like a little teapot filled with poison, we are not going to tip you gently, nether shall we pour thee delicately into a fancy cup. We are going to shatter you open and rub you out."

The warring angels also carry away the flatlined dragon. The warring angels speak to Chris and Bill, "We'll let you watch."

Chris and Bill's vision telescope away from their bodies, like in a clairvoyant experience, and follow the warring angels that arrested Balor and company, all the way to the throne room. Yahweh, Yeshua, and the wise-man-apparition are together, and Balor and company are held in ropes, chains and bonds, and locked in a chamber.

Chris and Bill's vision are returned to their bodies. There are warring angels everywhere, clashing swords, shields and wands with multitudes of devils, and carrying people out of the world. It appeared that some people were being rescued, but others were being arrested. One of warring angels grabs Chris, still holding the orb that Clarissa's spirit is trapped in, and Bill, shouts, "We're ready," and flies off carrying them to the throne room of Heaven.

Chapter

16

It's the day of reckoning. The Earth, the astral
plane and the plane of outer darkness alike had been
evacuated of all souls, and they now stand, great and
small, living, dead, and undead, in the throne room
which has been enlarged beyond measure. Yahweh,
Yeshua, and the wise-man apparition are sitting at what
looks like a court bench. The wise-man apparition
says, "The grace of God that brings salvation had
indeed appeared to all entities, whether in Heaven,
Earth, and under the Earth, and all have received it
except they which knowingly and willingly took sides
with *Wrong Itself*."

Having full access to His own *Akashic Record*,
which is also called *the Book of God's Remembrances,
the Scroll of Zoe, and the Book of Life*, it doesn't take
long for Yahweh to prove John Adramalech Balor, his
wizards and witches including his liaison Tammy
McLillith the *Scarlet Whore of Babylon*, the dragon
which is also *the seven-headed hydra of blasphemies*,
and all the daemons guilty as charged. Yahweh says,
"According to common sense, an open and shut case.
Yeshua, I'll need that key."

Yeshua says, "Be very careful. We don't know all

the details about what will happen after you do this, but here's the key." He pulls out a black key with a pentagram on it's handle, and hands it to Yahweh.

Yahweh says, "I've got to do this quickly, we have no choice. They will obliterate us if they roam free here." He places the key in a hatch door hidden in the back of the throne room. As the door opens, it reveals a blazing inferno stinking of sulfur, and these wicked rulers are thrown in head long into a bottomless abyss of fire, along with millions of daemons, evil sorcerers and also their human cronies and bootlickers. Yeshua lays his hands on the dead seven-headed dragon, and it starts to come back to life, one head at a time. Quickly, Yeshua and fourteen warring angels throw the seven-headed dragon into the fire chamber. The door is quickly locked before anyone can hear their screams of torment.

Chris holds up the orb that holds Clarissa Methodiste. Mark and Joey approach quickly. They lay their hands on it and Yeshua joins them. The black orb breaks like a balloon pop, and Clarissa falls to the floor, gasping with relief, "Oh Christopher Joshua? Is that you? Dad? Joey? I thought I'd never see any of you again!"

Yeshua is carrying what looks like a long brass stick, with a hard, dark stone on it. He opens the fiery chamber, and heats the stone, holding the door onto its stem to make sure nothing gets out of the chamber. He points to Melissa, "Come here."

Tabitha weeps in terror, "It's because my mom has *the Mark of the Beast*, isn't it?"

Yeshua asks, "Chris, do you forgive your dad and his for all they have done?"

"Yes. Will you?"

Yeshua asks, "Noah, do you forgive your mother and father?"

"Yes. Will you?"

Yeshua asks, "Tabitha, do you forgive Melissa for what she's done?"

"Yes, I do. Now, will you, Yeshua? And Yahweh?"

Melissa says, "I wanted nothing to do with this *Mark of the Beast*! The hospital put it in without my consent!"

Yahweh says, "Yet part of the essence of the beast was in your heart long before the mark was made!"

Yeshua pulls the heated stone from the chamber of

fire, and quickly closes the door. The heat from the stone is enough to increase the temperature of the whole atmosphere by about 20 degrees, immediately. Yeshua touches the burning stone to Melissa's forehead. Melissa screams.

The *Omnibus Civil Stability Chip*, that is, *the Mark of the Beast*, falls out of Melissa's head as that part of her skull is melted by the heat of the touchstone. Yeshua picks it up, opens the door to the chamber of fire, throws the *OCS* chip into the fire, slams the door, and heals Melissa's forehead with the touch of His hand. Where the *OCS* chip was, is now what looks like a white marble stone. As it cools down, it turns into an eye in her forehead. A minute later, it closes, sinks back into her head, and is covered by new skin.

Chris says, "Something tells me that the war is not over yet, but I don't know what it is."

The disciples attempt to re-light the *Menorah of Shalom*. It just won't light. *The Witch of Endor* walks in, and addresses the crowd, "Test my spirit now, I must tell a prophesy!"

Chris gazes into her eyes, and knows, "Yes, speak it real, and speak it well," then says so.

The stars in the sky are getting noticeably dimmer. The shadow scorpions over the lake buzz in excitement and anticipation.

Samuel says, "Yes, also."

The message projected by the *Amulet of Unity* on the stone table suddenly gets much brighter, **"Remember them that are in bonds, as bound with them; and them which suffer adversity, as being yourselves also in the body."** And underneath, **"Yes, hear her. What the enemy meant for evil, I have taken for good. What I have cleansed, call ye not unclean."**

The Witch of Endor speaks, "Although the man John Adramalech Balor, and all his human followers, have been cast into the abyss of fyre, the spirit of the *Archdaemon Adramalech* yet endures, by means of the *Embabylonian Knotweed*. This destiny too horrible to tell, that I have shown Chris and Bill, and confirmed twofold by the *Still Small Light within the Core of the Dark*, within and without, is still on its way to happening. The evil that inspired John Adramalech Balor is able to prevail without him."

Melissa comes in.

The Witch of Endor continues, "Melissa, it's you! You saw it! Tell us about the *Embabylonian Knotweed.*"

Melissa answers, "Oh, yes. *Embabylon* is rising, and its infernal weed is spreading through bubbles in the space-time continuum, so well hidden that even from here we won't see it coming until it has strangled the universes, even ours eternal in Heaven. It started in the very tree stump from *Daniel*'s prophecy, although none could see it. For at the fall of Babylon, its unseen and even more evil twin arose. Even the image of the Lord is transformed into that of a creepy thing and hateful bird."

The Witch of Endor continues, "Yes, I can see it now!"

On the surface of the darkened lake, the *shadow scorpions* are scurrying as if they are startled. Green stalks are starting to grow out of the water, at about an inch per hour, almost fast enough to watch them grow in real time.

Noah and Joshua show an *Akashic record* memory of when they used to play in this lake when six of the seven suns were still up.

Chris says, "No time for reminiscing now!" and starts to cry with traces of blood, and Bill chatters his teeth. Mark, Joey, Nathan, Ethan, Mikey, Tabitha, Noah and Joshua breathe extremely slowly, and hold their teeth tightly together, and are flinching their eyes, jugular veins throbbing in terror.

Samuel and the *Witch of Endor* wave their arms together, and a vision into the future is projected for all to see, of the growing knotweed-like plant that Melissa saw. It is seen filling the universes, even encroaching into every nook and cranny of Heaven.

The Witch of Endor continues, "This vile plant hath a will of its own. *Embabylon*'s oppression spreads through its roots, thorns, and tentacles, and though the leaves be heart-shaped, this vile bush will take vengeance in spades upon all that once was good and true, even here in Heaven, or, as we may one day say, what used to be Heaven. After the Earth is done burning down to the bare magma with the force of fifty times the whole world's nuclear arsenal, by the *Great Seven Phials of the Completion of the Wrath of God*, for it is the only way we could stave off this inter-dimensional *Embabylonian Knotweed*, we must return to the realm of *Malkuth*, relocating even the throne room, and land on Earth with the *Cubic City*. From there we may be secure enough to plan our next move."

Chris asks, "A 1500 mile cube. The Earth is more than ten times that. Isn't that still way too small for a physical reincarnation of all the ages that ever lived?"

Rick says, "We have found ways around that. Those not needed for critical tasks in our war could wait it out in created spaces, just like we did in the *Dungeons of Britnoitula*. In my opinion, no more far-fetched than making a doorway out of one pearl. The time dilation will be quite useful, since a thousand years is a long time for a busy-wait."

The wise-man apparition picks up the *Menorah of Shalom*. Muscular-looking angels are carrying many items from the room, including the stone table with the animated armor parts. Yeshua beckons the crowd down a path, through a dark forest, and says, "Keep your eyes straight ahead."

As they walk, strangely colored lights and buzzing sounds appear to the side. Bill's eyes shift, and he feels a deep cold chill. Suddenly he can't move. Chris grabs Bill's shoulder, and pushes his head back toward the path, and yells, "Keep your eyes on Him!"

The trek continues through the dark forest, until they reach a glowing wall so tall that its top is way out of sight. In front of them is a wall made of polished jasper. Looking way up, what seemed over a hundred miles, there is a line where the jasper changes to sapphire. People in line seem to disappear into a glowing white round hole in the wall.

As Bill reaches the hole, he can now see that he's in a labyrinth, and the walls are all solid jasper. Following the line crowd led by Yeshua, they travel the maze and reach a staircase to the second floor. The walls are all solid sapphire. The march continues up to the twelveth floor, each staircase over a hundred miles tall, and each floor's maze walls of a different solid gemstone. Unlike the hallway-mazes of the other floors, the top is all wide open, and the ceiling clearer than glass, as if it were air.

The floor begins to spin rapidly. Everything is engulfed in a flash of red light. The wise-man apparition waves a wand, and everyone in the multitude is resized to one inch tall. The wise-man apparition says, "So we can fit comfortably. Better than making you guess which cupcake to eat, don't you think?"

Bill asks, "A strange shape for a space ship."

The wise-man apparition replies, "And more. This top floor would be the bridge. The mazes are for our security. There are also eleven other doors. The fires from the seven phials have purified the crust of the planet, and burned off all the *Embabylonian Knotweed* for about 33 million miles into space. Not terribly far in astronomical terms, but almost reaching Mars. The smoke puts up a barrier that the weed can't penetrate, but it will only last about a thousand years. Since we are all immortal now, it will grow back in and come for us if we are not successful in defeating the root cause of it. Don't the arrangements of the twelve gates at the base of this cubic labyrinth remind you of the numbers on an analog clock? Each is actually a portal to an age. Christopher Joshua, follow me."

The wise-man apparition leads Chris down the twelve floors of the maze, then up again to a well-hidden room in the eleventh floor, reached from a completely different path through the mazes. There is a glowing translucent orb, flowing in many colors, with a spinning hourglass inside. He says, "This is the arrow of time. To activate those gates, we must break it. More about this later. For now," and pulls out an *Akashic orb* labeled *"Earthly Life Record: Christopher Raphael Joshua,"* and hands it to Chris. "This will help you remember. Because you have seen time rips, recalling these experiences may provide clues on how to make it happen. I'll let you open it up and tell your story. I already know it all from my vantage point, but I need to hear it in your own voice to find the power we will need, because, when you tell it to me in your own voice, that *Still Small Light within the Core of the Dark* will be behind you."